PLOT SUMMARY

Now a fugitive—having been framed for murder—Special Agent Nathaniel Arkin, a disgraced former intelligence officer, continues his pursuit of a shadowy group he suspects of orchestrating an international assassination campaign targeting charismatic, fledgling fanatics—future Hitlers and bin Ladens—just as they emerge from obscurity, before they are capable of instigating mass murder. The barest of clues lead him on a desperate quest to hunt down the hidden ringleaders of the conspiracy and find evidence that might ultimately clear his name. As he goes along, Arkin begins to wrangle with the question of whether the group should, in the interest of the greater good of humanity, be left to its philanthropic but murderous ways.

Praise for *The Shadow Priest*
"This is a great beach read."
— *USA Today Network*

Praise for *Chasing the Monkey King*
"Entertainment so involving you won't realize you're being educated too."
— *Coast Weekend*

Praise for D.C. Alexander
"Alexander's characters are complicated, and whether his protagonists are interrogating suspects or shooting the breeze with one another, they do it with cocky aplomb."
— *The Kitsap Sun*

THE SHADOW PRIEST — BOOK TWO

ISBN-10: 1981219250
ISBN-13: 978-1981219254

Printed in the United States of America

ACKNOWLEDGMENTS

For invaluable assistance, advice, and encouragement along the way, I owe a debt of gratitude to Holly Pemberton, Ellen Nason, and Jamie Mingus.

I am also grateful to many authors and literary mavens for their priceless guidance over the years, including Sue Grafton, J.A. Jance, Kevin O'Brien, P.J. Alderman, Dr. Allen Wyler, Mike Lawson, Jane Porter, David Long, Greg Bear, Mark Lindquist, John J. Nance, Kelley Eskridge, Julie Paschkis, Jennie Shortridge, Dia Calhoun, Nancy Horan, Robert Dugoni, Nancy Pearl, Jess Walter, Stephanie Kallos, Royce Buckingham, Layton Green, and Rose O'Keefe.

For Holly and Haley

THE SHADOW PRIEST

BOOK TWO

The whole problem with the world is that fools and fanatics are always so certain of themselves, and wiser people so full of doubts.

—*Bertrand Russell*

ONE

The three men—two in their 70s, one in his late 30s—sat staring at each other on computer screens in rooms thousands of miles apart, brought together by an encrypted videoconference link. The oldest of the three sat utterly mute and motionless in a motorized wheelchair in a room of whitewashed stone walls while the other two spoke.

"I just decoded River Team's last signal," said the younger of the two speakers.

"And?"

"It's graded 'urgent.'"

"And?"

"Apparently Target River Three managed to find documents that reveal the location of Praetorian Station."

"How did we let that happen?"

"It hardly matters now."

"It always matters."

"We'll get it sorted. As a more immediate concern, the team is requesting permission to take preventive measures."

The elder of the two speakers looked down for a moment, as if studying his hands. "I don't suppose they gave you any detail as to exactly why they think it's absolutely necessary that they—"

"All indications are that, for the moment, River Three is the only outsider known to have knowledge of Praetorian Station's location. But it is clear that he intends to disperse this information as soon as he gets to his office tomorrow morning, if not before he brushes his teeth tonight."

The elder of the two speakers went quiet again, turning to look out a window. "What is River Three's name?" he asked at last.

"Encryption or not, according to our teleconference procedures, that you drafted by the way—"

"I asked you what his name is."

"Don't do this to yourself again."

"Tell me."

A pause. "Pratt. His name is John Pratt."

"And?"

"And he's a young DCI agent. He has a wife and four small children."

The elder of the two speakers closed his eyes and exhaled as though punched in the stomach, his face still turned away from his videoconference camera.

"This is our last chance to get the toothpaste back in the tube," the younger man continued. "Either that, or we close down Praetorian Station, sanitize, and build new identities for—"

"I can see that."

For the better part of a minute, no one spoke. Finally, the elder of the two speakers faced the camera again. "Decision?" he asked before holding his breath.

For the first time, the mute old man in the motorized wheelchair moved. He lifted his pale, bony index finger from the control joystick of his chair and held it there, pointed, for just a moment before letting it drop back down. The gesture was hardly noticeable, but the other two men were watching for it.

The elder speaker exhaled and nodded slowly. "So be it. Signal the team to proceed.

THREE MONTHS LATER

TWO

Special Agent Bill Morrison sat atop his dark brown stallion on a wide open, brush-dotted New Mexican plateau roughly 25 miles southeast of the Four Corners—the point where the borders of Arizona, Utah, Colorado, and New Mexico meet. It was a cold but sunny day with a steady 10-knot wind blowing down from the north. There wasn't a cloud to be seen in any direction. Three miles ahead, towering nearly 1,600 feet above the desert floor, loomed Shiprock—the jagged, eroded remnant and throat of a 27 million-year-old volcano. Morrison would ride no closer out of respect for Navajo beliefs that Shiprock was a holy place of sorts. Indeed, according to one legend, Shiprock had once been a massive bird—an agent of the Great Spirit—that first brought the Navajo to the region, helping them flee warlike tribes that were assaulting their former homelands in the North. The Navajo still called it "the winged rock."

Even at this distance Shiprock was awe-inspiring. Morrison always thought it looked something like a medieval cathedral. The Notre Dame of the American desert southwest.

Morrison had acquired his horse while deployed on military service overseas, bending a few regulations and calling in a huge favor with a drinking buddy who was a charter cargo plane pilot in getting it shipped back to the U.S. Until recently, he'd thought it was an Arabian—in part because of an odd brand on the animal's flank that looked to Morrison like a modified Arabic letter. But an equine vet he'd taken riding the previous month, in a ham-handed and ultimately unsuccessful campaign to convince her to date him, had corrected his mistaken belief and explained that his horse was instead a Habash— an ancient, rugged, and uncommon breed found in the most remote and mountainous parts Central Asia. Habash horses were famed for their use in Buzkashi—an Afghani game somewhat akin to polo, the most notable difference being that in place of long mallets and a white plastic ball, the horse-mounted players used their bare hands and a headless, disemboweled goat carcass.

Morrison was at the turnaround point of a 30-mile ride—no problem for a strong horse like his. He'd parked his truck and trailer on the side of a rutted dirt road that ran along an undeveloped stretch of the San Juan River, ridden upstream to where the tiny Chaco River flowed into it, then followed the Chaco south until he emerged on the wide-open plain that Shiprock stood upon a few miles to the west. He pulled a canteen from his saddlebag and took a long, welcome drink of water.

He'd taken the long ride to clear his head. To meditate on what was to come. It had been a rough week. He'd driven thousands of miles to covertly reunite his good friend Nate Arkin—a federal agent turned federal fugitive—with his dying wife, Hannah. Once Hannah succumbed, after a long and grueling battle with cervical cancer, Morrison assisted in Arkin's escape from the area and made arrangements for Hannah's funeral. All of this on top of his regular work schedule. And he'd managed it all while under surveillance. He was definitely under surveillance by the U.S. Marshall Service and FBI—who had been hoodwinked into thinking that Arkin was a murderer. He was also probably under surveillance by a homicidal, ideological group of assassins that Morrison and Arkin referred to as "the Priest's group." A group that Arkin originally thought had been formed by a lapsed Jesuit priest named Collin Bryant. A group that Arkin believed was led by Roland Sheffield—a man who'd been Arkin's mentor, father figure, and boss years earlier when they'd both worked at DCI—the Directorate for Counter Intelligence—a post-9/11 inter-agency counterterrorism task force based out of the U.S. Department of Justice in Washington, D.C.

The previous week, Morrison and Arkin had flushed Sheffield from his hiding place in Eugene, Oregon, where he was living under an assumed name while working as a professor of sociology at the University of Oregon. In the process, they'd drawn out and then facilitated the demise of Andrej Petrović—a psycho Serbian-Canadian artist, sniper, and assassin who for years the Priest's group had been dispatching to murder charismatic extremists of every banner all over North America.

It had been four days since Hannah's passing. It had been three since Arkin, somber and heartbroken, had departed for the Pacific Northwest on a quest for evidence that would exonerate him from an exceptionally clever frame-up—carrying nothing more than a water bottle, a bag of granola, a medium-duty backpack stuffed with clothes, a compact one-man tent, a sleeping bag, and a burner cell phone Morrison had given him. Arkin skipped his wife's funeral because he knew people would be watching for him—people who wanted to either arrest or kill him. He rode away on an old Suzuki sport bike Morrison had borrowed from a friend over in Pagosa Springs. Morrison had given Arkin strict instructions to obey the speed limit and keep his helmet on to avoid any entanglements with law enforcement. But they both knew that, in the unlikely event police attempted to pull him over, Arkin had a good chance of losing them given that the bike had a top speed of damn near 180 miles per hour.

Though he was physically and emotionally weary, Morrison knew his hardship didn't hold a candle to the ordeal Arkin had dealt with of late. Somehow, the Priest's group had managed to frame Arkin for murder and have federal law enforcement agencies label him a high-priority fugitive, all as his wife's health was failing, forcing Arkin to flee their hometown of Durango, Colorado. Forcing him to pursue Sheffield and Petrović to clear himself and to neutralize the threat they posed to himself and others. And while Petrović was now dead and Sheffield on the run, it was a good bet that the Priest's group was out there regrouping. Planning more murders. Still planning to kill Arkin—a man who knew too much about them.

As far as Arkin and Morrison could tell, the Priest's group was a band of killers that had penetrated the upper echelons of the U.S.

intelligence and federal law enforcement communities. Some were former military. Some were no doubt former spies or spymasters. They seemed to be very well-trained in the covert arts. Arkin believed they were motivated by an ostensibly benevolent goal—to pre-emptively save the world from future Hitlers and bin Ladens. But their methods were extrajudicial, centered on assassinating particularly charismatic extremists—any nut job with a growing following—before the extremists grew strong enough to wreak murderous havoc. And anyone who got in their way or threatened them, intentionally or by accident, got taken out. It didn't matter whether they were good or bad. John Pratt was one such victim. A good man. A husband and father of four beautiful young children. A friend. Morrison swore they'd have to step over his own dead body before they tried to kill Arkin too. He wasn't about to stand by and lose another friend.

THREE

That same evening, 1,200 miles away, having ducked under a double line of police crime scene tape, Arkin poked through the burned, mostly collapsed remains of what had been Sheffield's large house on a hillside toward the south end of Eugene, Oregon. It was dark out, but he wore night vision goggles as he poked around in the charred debris with a discarded broom handle, searching for anything that might give him a better idea of where the Priest's group was located and where Sheffield had gone. The lot was surrounded by dense vestiges of Pacific Northwest coastal rainforest, so Arkin wasn't overly worried about being spotted by a neighbor who might alert the police. Still, he kept one ear open and did his best to keep a low profile. His efforts kept him warm despite the cold, damp air.

There wasn't much left of the house. Though there were 80 or 90 square feet of scorched floor space flanked by remnants of wall in two opposite corners of the foundation, it had otherwise burned to the ground. Arkin had little doubt the fire had been deliberately set with copious amounts of kerosene—apparently one of the Priest's group's favored techniques for getting rid of problems such as a house full of evidence. Having arrived barely an hour earlier to find the house destroyed, Arkin wasn't expecting to find anything of value. But he had to try.

His hands, shoes, and pant legs were already filthy with soot. But he kept searching through the debris, moving aside pieces of charred wood, warped pieces of plastic melted beyond recognition, shards of smoked and broken glass, and partially-burned clothing. His back began to ache from being bent over as he picked through the detritus. But at last, in one of the somewhat intact corners, he lifted a scorched remnant of plasterboard to discover a five-by-seven photo in a simple gunmetal frame, protected by an unbroken pane of glass. Arkin took off his night vision goggles and turned on a small, red bulb LED flashlight he'd been carrying in his pocket to take a better look. In the photo, Arkin, Hannah, Sheffield, and Sheffield's late wife Claudia all stood on the deck of the Sheffields' beach house in North Carolina's Outer Banks, the warm orange light of the setting sun illuminating their smiling faces, a golden sand beach and crashing Atlantic surf in the distance behind them. Arkin remembered the trip well. Sheffield had invited him and Hannah down from D.C. for the weekend to celebrate after Arkin rolled up a terrorist cell that had been planning a shoulder-launched anti-aircraft missile attack at Andrews Air Force Base—presumably targeting Air Force One. It was a great weekend. The Sheffields had spoiled them with fine food and wine. The experience had cemented Arkin's view of Sheffield as someone he genuinely looked up to and cared about. As someone who genuinely cared about him—seemingly more than his own father had. And yet barely two weeks ago, Sheffield had shot him in the chest three times at close range with a small .32 caliber Berretta Tomcat, probably cracking a couple of his ribs in the process. If it weren't for his ballistic vest, he'd be dead. His ribs still hurt.

Arkin stood holding the photo, examining it in the red glow of his flashlight, puzzled. The same man who'd tried to kill him kept a framed photo of him and his wife in his house. What was he supposed to make of that?

*****

Meanwhile, back in Durango, Morrison ducked into a small bookshop on Main Avenue and chatted with the clerk—one of his ex-girlfriends—for a few minutes before heading to the office in back of the store to use the telephone. There, he dialed the number for the burner cell phone he'd given Arkin after having another friend buy it for him while on a weekend trip to Santa Fe.

"Connors residence," Arkin answered, using the first fake name that came to mind.

"Hola, pendejo."

"Hey," Arkin said, still transfixed by the photograph.

"Catch you at a bad time?"

"No, it's—I found a strange . . . ."

"What?"

"Nothing. Never mind."

"How was the ride north?"

"Uneventful. I'm tired. Had a bad night's sleep where I made camp down on the McKenzie River."

"Are you eating?"

"Don't have much of an appetite."

"You have to eat, Nate. Get yourself a nice bacon double-cheeseburger or something." Silence. "Anyway, got a few things to report."

"Yes?"

"First, I thought you'd like to know that there was a great turnout for Hannah's service. I didn't know you guys had so many friends."

"I don't. Everybody loved Hannah."

"Well. Yes." Morrison paused. "Anyway, there were four attendees who looked a little out of place. I recognized one from an inter-agency raid down in Chama last year. A U.S. marshal out of the Albuquerque field office. Decent guy. I took down the license plate numbers of the other three and ran them down on my magic law enforcement computer. All legit U.S. Marshal Service vehicles."

"*Four* U.S. marshals watching for me?"

"Hey, take it as a compliment. They respect your abilities."

"That's nice. But I'd just rather they bought me a beer instead of trying to put me in the bag at my wife's funeral. They aren't fooling around, that's for sure."

"At least there wasn't anyone there from the Priest's group. None of Sheffield's goons, far as I could tell."

"Maybe they're standing down and regrouping after we killed Petrović and flushed out Sheffield."

"That brings me to my next point. They aren't. I ran another check of ViCAP yesterday and came up with a hit in a suburb of Detroit, Michigan. A murder where the victim burned to death in a house fire set with kerosene. The victim was the editor-in-chief of a popular lunatic right-wing internet site for fabricated political news stories."

Arkin sighed. "A political extremist and popular fake

newsmonger. Sounds like the Priest's group alright. I guess that means time is still of the essence."

"If we really want to bother saving such jackasses."

"Let's not get too high on our ideological horses. Remember, one of the Priest's group's targets, Ted Wright, the First Nations activist in Alberta, has a 5-year-old daughter," Arkin said, thinking of a newspaper photo of Wright holding his little daughter's hand as they walked down the street with ice cream cones. A photo that Arkin had found on the internet while running a search on Wright after seeing the man's home address scribbled on a fax he'd found in a secret room in Petrović's Art Gallery in Vancouver, British Columbia. "Wright can't be *all* bad," he said, suddenly realizing that Wright could still be alive, and that if he was, he was probably still a target of the group. He had to be warned.

"Okay, Mr. Dalai Lama."

"Did you learn anything about the fax number?" Arkin asked, referring to one of the numbers he'd copied from a log of inbound and outbound faxes he'd also found in Petrović's secret room.

"Not much of use. I can't link the Valparaiso, Chile, fax number to a name or address. Not without the help of a Chilean phone service provider, which isn't an option."

"What about the one in Montserrat?"

Montserrat was a small island in the Leewards of the Caribbean Sea. A British Overseas Territory.

"Well, you already know that there was a big volcanic eruption on Montserrat in the late 1990s that destroyed the southern half of the island."

"Yes."

"I traced the fax number to an address."

"Great."

"Great, except for the fact that the address is for an office building in the dead center of the former capital city of Plymouth, which was destroyed in the eruption—buried in ash and pyroclastic flows."

"You sure the office wasn't maybe just outside of the destruction zone?"

"Not if Google Earth is to be believed. It's well within the volcanic wasteland."

"They haven't been rebuilding the town?"

"It's permanently abandoned."

14

"So, we can assume the bill for the number is being paid by someone elsewhere. And I wouldn't know how to trace it any further in a place like Montserrat."

"Neither would I."

They went quiet for a moment.

"What's the next move?" Morrison asked.

"There's nothing here in Oregon. Sheffield is long gone. They torched the house."

"Of course."

"There are leads to pursue in Washington, D.C. Killick's condo." Tom Killick had been the DCI director of operations who Arkin and Morrison had figured out was a mole—secretly an operative for Sheffield and the Priest's group. He had disappeared right along with Sheffield as soon as it became apparent that his cover was blown. "I'd like to take a look at Dragoslav Trlajic too."

"Who?"

"Dragoslav Trlajic. He was Killick's senior policy advisor at DCI. Apparently, he's still in D.C. Hasn't fled."

"What kind of heartless parents would name their kid Dragoslav? Might as well name him Lucifer."

"He also happens to be Serbian."

"Another Serb! I love it! Explains the demonic name. So—he's a Serb and he was Killick's high chamberlain. Those are two good reasons to give him a sniff, I suppose. Does he have the crazy Slobodan Milošević hair and bushy eyebrows?"

"I haven't seen him yet."

"But if Trlajic is part of the group, wouldn't he have flown the coop when Sheffield and Killick did?"

"Maybe. But then again, maybe he just doesn't have any reason to think we suspect his involvement. Maybe he thinks he's still in the clear."

"You're going to try to spy on a counterintelligence officer. Should be fun."

"Maybe he's just a POG," Arkin said, using an acronym for the Marine Corps slang expression *person other than grunt*—meaning someone in a support role as opposed to a frontline combat soldier.

"You going to ride your motorcycle all the way to D.C.?" Morrison asked. "And then, what, ride to Valparaiso, Chile, down the Pan-American Highway?"

D. C. ALEXANDER

"My testicles would fall off. No, I need a new name so that I can be mobile. A name that isn't listed as a federal fugitive in every law enforcement database from here to Timbuktu."

"You know somebody who can get you a new I.D.?"

"Not outside of federal law enforcement."

"What are you going to do? Steal someone's I.D.?"

"Borrow."

"You? Mr. By-the-book?"

"Curiously, I find myself feeling less restrained of late."

"Less restrained by what?"

"By the rules of engagement, to put it vaguely."

"So, the gloves are coming off?"

"Let's just say I'm being pragmatic. Weighing the ends against the means."

"You're starting to sound like Sheffield."

"Screw you."

Morrison didn't respond, but reflected on the fact that Arkin had always been a straight-laced agent. Had always adhered to a strict, self-imposed code of right and wrong. Now, it seemed, he was flashing a new willingness to cross the line—to use any means necessary to hunt down and destroy the group.

"What are you going to do now?" Morrison asked.

"Hunt my twin.""Huh?"

"Find someone who looks like me. Snag his passport."

"Good luck. Anything I can do on my end?"

"Not at the moment. I might need you to ride shotgun in D.C. in a couple of weeks. Think you can take time off from work?"

"I think I feel a bout of shingles coming on."

"Should have gotten that immunization they advertise in *Good Housekeeping* magazine."

"Coulda, woulda, shoulda—the loser's lament."

"Anything else?" Arkin asked.

"Unfortunately, yes, there is. A buddy of mine in the U.S. Marshall's Denver office told me that someone put a notation in your fugitive sheet saying that there was a good chance you could be in Eugene."

"Holy shit. How did—I guess they must have surmised that I'd search for Sheffield, or at least search his house."

"A good guess."

16

As if on cue, Arkin heard sirens. Multiple sirens. He paused to listen. They seemed to be heading in his general direction.

"I hear sirens."

"Coming your way?"

"Maybe," Arkin said, wondering if one of the neighbors was out walking the dog and spotted the beam of his flashlight through the trees.

"Get out of there. Call you in three days."

Arkin hung up as he ran for the forest at the back of the lot. He'd leave the way he came, down through the woods that flanked the hillside. Down to where he'd left his motorcycle lying on its side, hidden beneath the fronds of a cluster of giant sword ferns. The sirens might not have been for him. But he wasn't going to wait around to find out if they were.

FOUR

Late the next morning, 270 miles north of Eugene, Arkin pulled to the gravel shoulder of a forest-flanked road close to Seattle-Tacoma International Airport. He rolled the motorcycle into the trees and hid it in a thicket of salal bushes, then marched deeper into the woods. Soon enough, he found a soft, clear patch of ground under a dense canopy of firs beyond sight of the road and made camp. Within the hour, he located a nearby grocery where he spent some of his precious remaining cash—the use of a credit or ATM card was out of the question since they were easy to trace—on propane canisters, 50-cent bags of quick-cook Cajun beans and rice that were on a clearance sale, a lighter, and some basic toiletries. Back at camp that evening, he built a crude blind out of sticks and ferns to obscure the firelight of the stove, then cooked himself a simple dinner. As he finished, it began to pour rain. He withdrew to the shelter of the tent and was soon falling asleep to the pitter-patter of large droplets that consolidated in the fir needles above and fell onto the taught waterproof rainfly protecting his tent.

He woke once in the night, certain that he smelled Hannah's hair. The scent of plumeria, from a shampoo she'd used ever since discovering it on their first trip to Kauai. The sensation was so strong that he was sure he'd open his eyes to see her lying there next to him. But as he regained his wits, he remembered that she was gone. Still, he reached out into the chilly air and felt around in the darkness just to be sure. There was no one, nothing there. He ached to see Hannah's face. To feel the warmth of her arm lying against his as she slept. To just hear her breathing. Smell her hair. Things he once took for granted.

*****

The next morning, he set off for the airport on foot—knowing there'd be no free parking, and he wanted to conserve his cash— donning a baseball cap and pulling his hooded sweatshirt up around his face as best he could. It took him just about an hour to reach the terminal. Scanning the flight information screens, he took note of every international arrival that day. He found a table in a brightly-lit reception hall where he had a clear view of where passengers from international arrivals were disgorged from an escalator after leaving U.S. Customs. Taking stock of the positions of the various security cameras, he grabbed a discarded *Seattle Times*, kicked back, and did his best to look like somebody waiting to meet an arriving passenger, all the while keeping his face obscured by pages of the paper or turned away from the probing lenses.

As he waited, it occurred to him that it would be a good time to warn Ted Wright, the First Nations activist from Alberta, that he'd been targeted for assassination by the Priest's group. Warn him that he should run and hide, and take his beautiful little 5-year-old daughter with him. The first thing Arkin did was Google the man's name along with the words "first nations," looking for any sort of phone number or other contact information he could use to track the guy down. But within seconds, he learned his efforts were futile. The online version of the *Calgary Herald* newspaper had an article titled "RCMP to Investigate Killing of First Nations Activist." The accompanying photo was an old mugshot of Wright.

Arkin's heart pounded in his chest and his face grew hot as he pictured Wright's little girl, her smiling face turned up to look at her dad as they walked with their ice cream cones. Such helpless innocence. What would become of her? Did she have any relatives who might step forward to take care of her? Would she be taken away to live with a foster family of total strangers? Would she be handed over to the government foster care system? Would she fall prey to the neglect and abuse so common to such situations? It made Arkin furious. What could possibly justify such a killing? A killing with such consequences, such collateral damage for the innocent? The

Priest's group had to be stopped. And stopped soon, before they could orphan any more innocent children.

Two hours later, a gleaming Air France 777 pulled into a gate across the tarmac. Twenty minutes after that, haggard and bleary-eyed passengers began pouring from the top of the escalator. Arkin scanned each male face. The people came in waves as they were dropped by subways arriving from U.S. Customs every few minutes. After the eighth or ninth such wave, the flow petered out. He hadn't seen what he was looking for.

He waited for one more international arrival—a 747 from Taiwan—but met with similar disappointment. Deciding that if he stayed any longer he might pique the interest of security, he gave up for the day and made his way back to camp.

FIVE

Arkin followed a similar routine—choosing different spots in the airport in which to wait and changing up the combination of clothes and baseball caps he wore—for more than a week, subsisting off Cajun beans and rice. By day six, he never wanted to see another Cajun dish as long as he lived. To keep himself from getting conspicuously rank and filthy, he took to bathing, shaving, and washing his clothes in a relatively clean, clear, but ice-cold pool below a culvert that ran under a road in a heavily-wooded ravine a few hundred yards west of his camp. On one of the days it rained constantly, so he stayed put for fear that his arriving at the airport soaked to the bone would arouse suspicion. Why hadn't he thought to buy an umbrella?

He was getting sick of sitting on his butt in the woods, sick of sitting at the airport, sick of bathing in ditch water, sick of the smell of his food. His back hurt from sleeping on the ground night after night. His sleep was fitful, haunted by dreams of his dying wife. Of her terrible fear. Of his uselessness. His utter inability to help her.

Finally, on day eight of his vigil, Arkin saw what he was looking for. An exhausted looking male passenger coming off a British Airways 777 from Heathrow. Six-foot-two. Medium build. Dark hair. Not a dead-ringer for Arkin by any stretch, but close enough.

Arkin tracked the man to the light rail station—glad he wouldn't have to ask Morrison to trace a license plate—and boarded a train car adjoining the one the man boarded. The train wound its way down into the Duwamish River Valley, over into the Rainier Valley, then into a tunnel under Seattle's Beacon Hill neighborhood.   Arkin followed at a discreet distance as the man disembarked at Beacon Hill Station and walked east on McClellan Street, slowed by his rolling suitcase.   The man eventually turned south and went another block before ascending a short walkway to the door of a small bungalow. Arkin marked the house, noting its number out of the corner of his eye as he walked past.   It sat on a quiet residential side street.   It had an old-fashioned stand-alone mailbox out front and an alley behind. Perfect.

By that evening, Arkin had relocated his camp to another area of woods—broad-leaf maple, alder, and Douglas fir sheltering a dense undergrowth of Eurasian blackberry vines and fern—flanking the western slope of Beacon Hill.   Judging by the many well-worn footpaths and sheer quantity of debris, Arkin was sure the area often served as a refuge and temporary encampment for vagrants.   All the better.   He'd be less likely to draw anyone's attention in an area known as a haven for squatters.   Just the same, he did the best he could to locate his tent out of sight of either the nearby homes or anyone who might wander along one of the meandering trails.

That night it rained hard.   The wet pavement made Interstate 5, unseen but just below his camp, all the louder.   He hardly slept.   And he was running out of food.   Days of meager, rationed portions of quick-cook Cajun beans and rice had his subconscious preoccupied with nourishment, so that when he did manage to sleep, he dreamt of things like grilled Argentine skirt steak, spaghetti with browned butter and mizithra cheese, pepperoni pizza, and caramel cake.

Up before dawn, Arkin made his way back to the house of the man he'd followed from the airport.   Under cover of the predawn darkness, and after a couple of awkward false starts, he managed to hide himself in a 10-foot-high, 4-foot-deep wall of English laurel hedge fronting a yard a half block up and across the street.   There, he waited and watched.   Just under two hours later, the man emerged from his house and headed north, presumably back toward the light rail station for his morning commute to work.   Waiting until the man was well out of sight, Arkin struggled free of the hedge, crossed the street, and circumnavigated the block, eventually entering the alley that ran up its middle.   Scanning as he walked, he was reasonably certain nobody had eyes on the alley.   He hopped a short chain-link fence behind the target house, strolled up to the back of it, and found an unlatched old double-hung bathroom window. He lifted it and crawled in.

As he'd hoped, the man hadn't unpacked, but had left his open suitcase on the floor of his bedroom. On a small desk in the adjoining room, he found the man's passport. William Cassady, born a mere three months after Arkin. And the photo could hardly have been better. He pocketed it, then scanned the desk for credit card applications. No dice. But to his happy surprise, he found the man's Social Security card among a rubber-banded stack of business and grocery store club cards. Perfect.

He made his way to the kitchen to burgle food. Simple things, dust-covered things—things in the back of cupboards that probably wouldn't be missed. A big bag of jasmine rice. Cans of corn, beans, and chili. An old, surely stale, half-consumed jar of instant coffee; a small indulgence. He stuffed the food into doubled-up grocery bags he found in Cassady's pantry, rifled through the bathroom cabinets to find two bars of soap, then headed back to camp.

SIX

Over the next three days, Arkin surveilled the street to ascertain the usual time of mail delivery, and to steal a "pre-approved" credit card application from Cassady's mailbox. The first one that came offered a ludicrously high interest rate, but also promised a high maximum balance. "Sorry about this, Mr. Cassady," Arkin said aloud as he filled out the application back in his tent.

The next day, Arkin hiked into downtown Seattle and made his way over to the gleaming new central library. He got hold of a computer and did more searching for the Chilean phone and fax numbers he'd recovered in Petrović's macabre Vancouver art gallery. Nothing more useful came up.

Damn.

Six days later, Arkin intercepted the new credit card in Cassady's mailbox and—once again using the internet-linked computers at the Seattle Central Library—used it to buy a one-way ticket to Reagan National Airport in Washington, D.C. the next day. Knowing full well he'd be creating a monster headache for poor Cassady, he selected the cheapest flight he could find, even though it was a red-eye with two plane changes and would take five hours longer than quicker but far more expensive options.

Feeling that he was at last making progress, he took a long celebratory walk around downtown Seattle, admiring its beautiful setting, its views out over Elliot Bay to the distant Olympic Mountains, its eclectic, lively public market where friendly merchants of its many stalls offered him nourishing free samples of hot clam chowder, crepes, sausages, cheeses, and fruits.

The next evening, a dark and dreary Pacific Northwest Monday, Arkin, traveling as Mr. William Cassady of Seattle, Washington, passed through TSA security without so much as a second glance and boarded a Boeing 737 for the first leg of his zig-zagging 10-hour journey to Washington, D.C.

SEVEN

Morrison slumped in his chair, staring down at the Animas River out his office window, unable to work, obsessed with figuring out a way to help Arkin. Given that he had a full-time job as a Special Agent for ATF, and given that he'd already taken a week off to help Arkin go after Sheffield in Oregon, he couldn't just up and head to the Pacific Northwest to rendezvous with Arkin again—especially if he was going to try to concoct an excuse to meet Arkin in Washington, D.C. But maybe there was something he could do from Durango. Maybe there was a way he could at least obtain some useful information that could help Arkin in his quest. What would Arkin most need? Identities and locations of the Priest group's operatives? Details of its command structure? Information on pending operations? Sure. But how the hell could Morrison get his hands on any of that?

Then an idea occurred to Morrison that made him sit up straight. The group had obviously been monitoring the various cell phones Arkin had used over the past few weeks. And its operatives were so professional and thorough that Morrison had a pretty strong suspicion they were monitoring his phones too. He picked up his phone and dialed the number of a cell phone Arkin had carried up until a week ago when he dumped it after deducing that it was compromised and being tracked. Morrison hung up before it rang. Too obvious. He picked up his phone again and dialed the office line of Detective Cornell, over in Cortez, who he figured had already punched out and gone to the tavern to watch his beloved UNM Lobos basketball team take on Brigham Young. To Morrison's great satisfaction, the call went straight to voicemail.

"Cornell, it's your number one fan, Bill Morrison. Listen, I have a printout with the names and addresses Arkin asked us to find. If you get this message and want me to read them to you, call me after hours because I don't have them at work. Got 'em stashed in my barn in case any of these assassin jokers breaks into our offices." He hung up. Was it still too obvious? Would the group smell a trap? Maybe. But maybe not. A smile broke out across his face. Then he ran for the door.

EIGHT

He'd seen no activity in or around the cabin since arriving more than two hours earlier. It would have been better if other operatives had stayed behind in Durango to tail subject River Two so that they could confirm his whereabouts. Regardless, he was sufficiently confident no one was home.

It took him more than 10 minutes to creep down to the barn on the back of the lot, utilizing all available concealment. It was dark, but he was taking no chances. River Two was known to have ATF-issued night vision gear.

As he approached the back door to the barn, he pulled up a cuff of his black BDUs, drew a small .38 semiautomatic from an ankle holster, and reached for the knob. He tried to turn it. Locked. He holstered his gun, took a tiny lock pick from a thigh utility pocket, and went to work. Before long he had the lock sprung and, gun in hand once again, was slowly pushing the door open, poised to stop at the first sign of a squeak.

When it was open just wide enough, he slipped through sideways, closed the door behind him, switched on a tiny pen light that cast a dim red beam, and scanned the interior. A set of cabinets lined the opposite wall, hung above a long wooden workbench. One of the cabinets stood out. It appeared to be made of steel, and its door had a lock on it. The natural place to start his search.

He holstered his gun, then began to tiptoe toward the locked metal cabinet. Halfway across the barn, he caught the faintest scent of soap. Soap a man would use. Old Spice. Then he heard the telltale clap of a Taser.

NINE

"I have to admit, I just love gadgets," Morrison said to the Japanese-looking man bound to the iron sewer outflow pipe in his basement as he stood staring at the smartphone in his hand. "This latest app I got lets me turn the lights on and off in my house, even if I'm a thousand miles away. I could be in India and do it. It's incredible what they come up with these days, isn't it?"

Morrison and his captive occupied a back corner of the concrete-walled basement that he'd partitioned off with bare bed mattresses, sofa cushions, and cardboard storage boxes piled to the well-insulated ceiling. Even if someone showed up at his front door—which was unlikely given that he lived in the middle of nowhere and it was the middle of the night—they'd never hear the screaming. The man sat on the floor, shoeless and in his underwear, with his legs splayed out in front of him and his feet handcuffed around the steel leg of a heavy workbench.

"Why am I talking about my smartphone, you're wondering? Partly because I just think it's so cool. But also, I want to let you know from the get-go here that I've adjusted this app to turn on just one circuit here," he said, gesturing to a small table on which sat a pair of needle-nose pliers and a coiled-up extension cord—the end of which had been stripped of insulation to expose bare copper wires that hung across the gap and led up to the man's ears, around which they were wrapped and held fast by a headband of duct tape. The opposite end of the cord was plugged into an old-fashioned manual voltage regulator. "In short, I can zap you from anywhere in the world. And that's relevant because I'm going to leave at times to go and verify the truth of what you tell me. Needless to say, if you lie, well...." He nodded toward the extension cord again.

The man had been looking at him. But hearing Morrison's threat, his line of sight drifted off, seeming to re-center on something beyond the walls of the makeshift torture chamber.

He speaks English, Morrison thought. *And he's trained in interrogation resistance. He's prepping. Trying to detach.*

"Something else you should know," he said. "I don't go in for all that polite stuff like water boarding and loud music when you're trying to sleep. My methods are Russian. Dark Ages Russian. Though really, Russia is still more or less in the Dark Ages if you ask me. But I digress. These first tricks I'm going to use were actually taught to me by a couple of friends in the Afghan Northern Alliance. And they learned them, in turn, from the good old Russians themselves, who were more than happy to teach my friends through experience."

The man still stared through the wall, seeming not to hear.

"You and I both know that no matter how hard you try to detach, your subconscious is still registering what I say. Recording it. Priming your conscious mind with alarm. With the seeds of terror." As he said this, Morrison took hold of the pliers. "And you and I also know that Russian methods work. All that talk about torture not being an effective way of obtaining accurate information is softie liberal nonsense, isn't it? You're going to give me the information I want. And you know it."

As he said, "know it," he tore the nail of the man's pinky toe out with the pliers, prompting a scream of pain the man did his best to quickly contain. Blood poured from the wound.

"I'll be honest, I'm not big on torture. At first, the idea troubled me. But then I thought, what if the situation was reversed? Would you think twice about torturing me? Did y'all think twice before you blew Pratt's brains out in front of his wife and kids? No, probably not. And the truth is, I'd do anything for Nate. I *will* do anything to help him. In that equation, your life isn't worth any more to me than that of a trout I would catch, gut, and cook for dinner. And truth be told, at the end of the day, aside from caring about my friends, I seem to be turning into a sort of nihilist. So, screw it," he said as he turned the dial and flipped the toggle switch on the voltage regulator, sending a current up the wires to the man's ears, prompting another glass-shattering scream.

"There's a taste. You go ahead and think about things while I go make myself a midnight snack. I think I'm going to have a salami sandwich on rye bread. A little mustard and mayo. Maybe a cold beer. See you in ten? Okay, then."

With that, Morrison went upstairs. Unsettled by what he'd done—what he still had to do—he had no intention of eating. Instead, he went up to his second- floor bathroom and splashed cold water on his face. Then he retrieved a fresh pouch of leaf chew tobacco from a cabinet in his kitchen, stuffed a golf ball-sized wad of it into his cheek, and sat down on a rocker on his front porch to contemplate his plan of interrogation. He could tell by looking at the man that he wasn't going to break quickly or easily. He might let himself scream, but he wasn't going to give Morrison anything until considerable time had passed. Maybe up to a week. But Morrison didn't have a week. He was going to have to be brutal. The thought made his stomach turn, which caught him off guard. After all, he'd killed people before. Quite a few people, in fact. But it had almost always been from a distance. Shooting someone from 200 yards away was an altogether different thing than torturing and mutilating someone at close range. Seeing the terror and anguish in their eyes.

He took a deep breath and willed his mind's eye to a vision of his most recent camp on the high plateau near Mount Oso. A deep blue sky. A fresh dusting of snow on the aspens. A roaring bonfire. Just him and his horse.

*****

Twenty minutes later, he removed the storage boxes and twin-size mattress that blocked the entrance he'd designed into his hastily-constructed torture chamber to reveal his captive contorted and slumped forward in an unnatural, almost impossible-looking pose. His skin had taken on a bluish hue. His underwear was down to his knees.

"Shit!" Morrison jumped forward and lifted the man's head by the hair to reveal his expressionless face, his eyes and mouth open. He checked the man's pulse. Nothing. He thought he smelled a hint of almonds so he bent closer to the man's lips to take a whiff. Cyanide. Perplexed, Morrison stepped back and tried to piece together what had happened. He noticed that a button on the front of the man's boxer shorts was newly broken, half of it missing. He pulled the other half off and examined it. It was chalky. It wasn't a real button at all, but a suicide pill disguised as one. Probably molded from potassium cyanide crystals and some sort of binding agent. But how had the man reached it when he was bound to the sewer outflow pipe, his hands cuffed behind his back? It seemed he'd somehow wormed and wriggled until he was able to slide his underwear partway down. Then he'd dislocated both of his own shoulders to give his torso just enough flexibility to bend over so that he could bite the cyanide button off his raised knees. Morrison stood staring, defeated but in awe. These people would do anything to protect their group. To safeguard their cause. No matter how extreme or ludicrous their actions seemed.

TEN

Upon landing at Reagan National Airport, just across the broad, brown Potomac River from Washington, D.C., Arkin used his burner smartphone to find the nearest thrift shop, which turned out to be a fair hike up into the southern fringes of Arlington, west of Fort Myer. There, he bought an outfit of worn, second-hand articles of clothing—shoes, pants, shirt, and insulated jacket—that were just shabby and ill-matched enough to be believable as the clothes of a homeless man. From there, he made his way back down to the Potomac where he fouled his hands in somewhat fetid mud on the riverbank and set to work giving his new outfit a convincing, smelly, but just tolerable patina of filth. Then he walked upriver, along the Mount Vernon Trail bike path, until coming to the Columbia Island Marina, in the very shadow of the Pentagon. Catching the locking door to the marina's public bathroom as someone left, he went in, dumped trash out of one of the wastebaskets, removed and turned its white plastic trash bag inside out, stuffed his fouled new outfit into the bag, wrapped it again in the trash bag from the other wastebasket, then stuffed the whole double-wrapped thing into his duffel with the clothes and toiletries he'd brought from Seattle. Back outside, he found a stand of trees in an out-of-the-way area of the island, just north of the Marina and on the edge of Boundary Channel. There, assured by the weather application on his smartphone that there was absolutely no rain in the forecast for the next several days, he hid his bag under a dense clump of brush and woodland debris. Then he crossed over the Potomac via the 14th Street Bridge and stopped at the massive, neoclassical

Jefferson Memorial for a drink of water, a snack, and a breather.

There were few tourists about. Chewing on a hunk of peppered beef jerky he brought all the way from Seattle, he sat on the marble steps of the memorial, staring out over the Tidal Basin under the stern gaze of a 19-foot-tall bronze Thomas Jefferson, pondering his next move. He'd check into a homeless shelter under a fake name come evening—part of his scheme to leave as little traceable evidence of his visit to D.C. as possible. But he was torn over what to do with his day. He could begin a cautious, extremely arm's-length surveillance of Dragoslav Trlajic. However, he'd be wise to wait for Morrison's assistance before taking a close look at the man.

Another idea had been gnawing at him—one that had been growing in the back of his mind for several days. The Priest—Father Collin Bryant—had grown up in nearby Baltimore, Maryland. A short train ride to the north. Granted, Arkin was all but sure that Bryant was long-dead, having drowned—accidentally, or on purpose—in the Mississippi River in 1974. All but sure that Bryant was nothing more than a phantom, a name used by the group to serve as a figurehead or perhaps a red herring for anyone investigating them. Still, something tempted Arkin to learn more about the man. Perhaps he still had family in the area. Perhaps someone could tell him something useful. After all, whether he was alive or dead, his story had, on some level, significant meaning to Sheffield's murderous group.

Turning to look at the statue of America's third president, Arkin wondered what Thomas Jefferson would make of a fanatic like Sheffield. They'd probably share a mutual admiration, given that Jefferson had been something of a fanatic himself. Indeed, Jefferson had been an ardent apologist for the Reign of Terror—the bloodbath instigated by maniacal leaders of the French Revolution. In Arkin's view, that meant Jefferson, like Sheffield, was someone who was all too ready to accept evil deeds as justified means to righteous ends. Yet in most classrooms, Jefferson was worshipped as one of the infallible gods of America's civil religion. It didn't make much sense to Arkin. But he knew he'd always be in the minority when it came to his views on many of the founding fathers. After all, nobody liked to find fault with their gods.

ELEVEN

"Torture?" Arkin asked Morrison over the phone as he sat on a marble bench next to the Washington Monument. "That's a little out of character for you, isn't it?"

"Desperate times. Anyway, you're the one who said the gloves were coming off in our last conversation."

"Yeah, but shit, Bill!"

"You're angry."

"Well, I mean, what are we becoming here?"

"Said the man who just broke into a man's house, stole his I.D., and applied for a credit card in his name."

"Please. Borrowing someone's I.D. isn't even on the same planet as torture."

"Look, I hardly got to touch the son of a bitch before he swallowed his suicide pill. Plus, necessity is the mother of shifting principles."

"Who are we if we let that happen?"

"Can you hear my eyes rolling over the phone line? We aren't talking about extracting information on hypothetical future terrorism or hypothetical anything. These people want to kill you. You, specifically. Right now. And don't give me any of that politically correct crap about torture not working. These people will never stop hunting you. They're murderers. They blew Pratt's brains out in front of his children. Think of his family. Think of what they've put *you* through."

Arkin paused. "I suppose I just don't want us to become what we despise, or whatever they say. We aren't Russians."

"You're being sensitive because I said you were turning into Sheffield the last time we spoke."

"No, I'm not," Arkin said, taking a breath. "What did you do with the body?"

"Oh, you'll love this. I printed out a performance sheet for Zastava rifles, tucked it in the guy's pocket, and dumped him in the bushes on the hillside opposite Pratt's house. When they find the body—which they will, given that I left his leg sticking out where it's visible from the main road—they'll link it to Pratt's killing. Who knows? Could cause trouble for the Priest's group if a clever investigator ends up involved. Plus, it will confound the group. They won't know what to make of it, assuming their operative didn't call his superiors with his plan to burgle my house."

"If he was as professional as the rest of them seem, he probably did."

"Well, whatever. It might make them stop and think before sending in another one of their goons."

"I don't know whether that's good or bad. Maybe next time they'll send five goons instead of one."

"Anyway, on a brighter note, looks like I'll be able to catch up with you in D.C. three days from now."

"You're kidding. How did you manage that?"

"Didn't even have to call in sick. The FBI is offering a training course on querying the new NCIC files. My boss thought it was very proactive of me to ask to go. I have a hotel room in Crystal City for five nights. Three nights for the class, and two more on my own dime to hang out for the weekend and see the sights—or so I told my boss. Anyway, I've got your back, as usual."

"I'm going to commission a life-size marble statue of you and erect it in my front yard."

"Yeah, yeah. Just buy me a beer with the money I loaned you when I get there."

"I'd be happy to buy you a beer with your money."

"By the way, had a buddy in Durango PD pull Dragoslav Trlajic's home address off a DMV database for you. Didn't want to do it myself in case anyone out there is watching my every move. Worried I'd set off alarm bells. Anyway, Trlajic lives in D.C., near Dupont Circle. Swann Street. Got a pen? I'll give you the number."

"I need something else too."

"What would that be?"

"Last known address for Robert and/or Adel Bryant, Baltimore. And/or current occupants of the same residence."

"The Priest's parents?"

"Es correcto."

"They must be dead by now."

"Yes. But Bryant had siblings. I imagine one of them inherited the house."

"Didn't you already interview all of them? Way back when you were leading a legitimate investigation?"

"Not all of them. There was one, a younger sister he was supposed to be very close to, who lived in Lesbos, Greece, at the time. Headquarters decided she was too far off the beaten path to bother with. Word was she was terminally single. If anyone inherited the family home, it was probably her. The other siblings have families established all over the country. None of them stayed in Baltimore."

"Can you blame them?"

"Hey now. I have a soft spot for Baltimore. Ate a lot of crab cakes on stakeout back in the day."

"Okay. But aside from giving yourself an excuse to get crab cakes, why bother talking to the Priest's sister? Didn't you decide the Priest was probably a long-dead red herring cover-story for Sheffield and his goons?"

"The sister is a loose end that has nagged at me for years. I'm in the area. Why not give her a look?"

"You're the boss. Do you still have the address of the Bryant family home somewhere in your office, or do I need to query it?"

"It should be in a mint green folder in my wall safe, assuming nobody has cracked it open and cleaned it out trying to find evidence of my whereabouts."

TWELVE

As he walked through the National Mall, between the Smithsonian National Air and Space Museum and National Gallery of Art on his way to Union Station, Arkin called the phone number he'd linked to the last known address of Robert and Adel Bryant, parents of Father Collin Bryant. A woman answered several rings after Arkin expected his call to go to voicemail, offering a strained "Bryant residence." She sounded obese—her voice labored and breathless. But there was a note of defiance in her tone that told Arkin he wouldn't get far by being pushy. Adopting a deferential manner, he established that the woman was a nurse who came by once a week to check on 'Ms. Lily'—Father Bryant's younger sister who had lived in Greece during Arkin's investigation six years earlier. Then he fed the woman his prefabricated story about being a doctoral student at Georgetown University who was doing his thesis on the long-term sociological impact of Jesuit parishes founded in poverty-level American communities during the 20th century. He was interested in learning about Bryant's parish given that Bryant was a Jesuit and his parish community was desperately poor.

Arkin took a MARC Penn Line commuter train through the urban decay and sprawl of Northeast Washington, toward Baltimore, observing the uniformly glum-looking riders who seemed hell-bent on not making eye contact with him. He switched to the light rail at Baltimore-Washington International Airport, then rode it through downtown Baltimore and north to a station near the Guilford neighborhood, where Father Bryant had grown up. It was an old neighborhood of giant trees and massive, architecturally stunning homes—many of which looked like manor houses of England's Oxfordshire countryside. Arkin marveled at their magnificence as he followed his phone's directions to Bryant's childhood home.

At last he came to it. It was a massive red brick affair, set well back from the street. A mansion in anybody's book. Georgian architecture. Three floors, four chimneys, a slate roof, five dormer windows on the top floor, a large glass conservatory on one end of the main floor, an ornate porte cochère on the other. A fitting home for the family of Bryant's father, who'd been the owner of a once formidable Atlantic fishing fleet. But the Atlantic fisheries were depleted, and the fishing fleets long gone. Arkin could tell just by looking at the house. It wasn't nearly as well-maintained as its neighbors. There were signs of neglect everywhere. Overgrown ivy crawling up the walls, half-covering some of the windows. Cracking paint. Masonry in need of a pressure washing and repointing. In the porte cochère, a 20-year-old blue Pontiac sedan sat looking forlorn. Overall, the property gave Arkin the impression of faded glory. A tarnished gem of a grander, more prosperous era.

Arriving at the front door holding a notepad and pen he'd purchased as props at a drugstore near the light rail station, he gave three solid knocks with a heavy antique door knocker bearing the face of Neptune, Roman god of the sea. After the better part of a minute, at which point Arkin was about to knock again, the door opened to reveal the ample frame of Mrs. Howard, the woman he'd spoken to on the phone. The nurse some Medicare-funded service had sent to look in on and treat Lily Bryant. For what, Arkin had no idea. He wasn't about to ask.

"Ms. Lily is in her room, but will be with you shortly. You can take a seat in the drawing room," she said, turning to lead Arkin down a dark wood-paneled hallway. The house smelled of ancient cigar smoke residue and dampness. Arkin didn't see a single light on anywhere—in the hallway they walked, in the side rooms they passed. All light came from the windows.

The passage eventually opened into a massive, high-ceilinged room that looked like something out of Downton Abbey. But the room was dusty and contained nothing more than rows of books lined up on high built-in shelves, a small table and lamp, a 5x7 rug, and two threadbare corduroy chairs that looked as if they could have come third-hand from Goodwill. There was no art on the walls, save for an amateurish watercolor of a single red rose in a silver vase. No couch. No other furniture. But there were floor-to-ceiling mirrors covering the entire wall opposite the bookshelves, which in Arkin's dime store psychologist mind meant that whomever had had them installed had the seemingly incongruous traits of narcissism together with low self-esteem. And, he thought, such traits are often handed down through generations, from parent to child. An unfortunate legacy. He wondered if Lily had inherited the same personality flaws that likely possessed the person who originally had the mirrors installed. Whatever the case, Arkin figured the room had once been the heart of the home, filled with artwork and fine furnishings. But it seemed that over time, the home's current owner, Lily Bryant—youngest of the 10 Bryant children—had sold everything off to fund other needs. He took a seat on the less suspect of the two chairs and waited.

After several minutes of sitting alone in the cavernous room, growing bored, Arkin rose and walked over to the bookshelves to examine the collection. All of the books were bound in fine gilt-edged leather. None of them looked as if they'd ever been touched. There were law books, books on birding, sailing, horsemanship, etiquette, and the cultivation of roses. Arkin wondered whether anyone in the Bryant family had ever had any genuine interest in such subjects, or whether the books were there merely for show.

Losing interest, he returned to his chair. As he sat down, the rug caught his eye. It was black, tan, and off-white, and had a pattern of paired diamond shapes within larger diamond shapes, enclosed by thick zig-zagging lines that ran along the outside edges. Arkin would have guessed it was Navajo if he hadn't already had the uncommon familiarity with Navajo weaving styles that practically comes via osmosis when one lives in the Four Corners area. It was surely Native American—perhaps from one of the Mexican tribes. It wasn't Navajo.

At long last, Lily Bryant shuffled into the room. She wore expensive but outdated clothes, and had obviously gone to great effort to fix her hair and makeup prior to Arkin's arrival. The combined effect was over-the-top. Where her lower arms extended from the silk of her blouse, Arkin could see deep, dark bruising of the sort people get from bumping against things when they are on prescription blood-thinning medications. Arkin stood.

"Hello Ms. Bryant. Thanks for taking the time to meet with me."

"Ms. Howard says your name is Grossman," she said as she sat down without saying anything along the lines of *welcome* or *please, call me Lily.*

"Yes ma'am. Dave Grossman."

"And you're a Jesuit. Sounds like a Jew name. And you're a doctoral candidate at Georgetown, and your dissertation could use information about my brother Collin, yes?"

"That's correct," he said, observing with revulsion that she was lighting an off-brand cigarette.

"Well, I must say I'm positively mystified as to how a Baltimore priest's experience starting an ill-fated parish in a dirt-poor black Kentucky town in the 1960s could have any relevance whatsoever in today's world," she said, staring at him with a penetrating gaze. "But I don't have any other obligations at this particular moment."

Taking that as the green light to begin his interview, Arkin thought up an innocuous question to break the ice. "Have you lived here your whole life?" he asked, already knowing the answer.

"I lived in Paris for several years. Then Ibiza. That's in Spain. Then in the Greek Isles. I come back when they beg me."

"For what?"

"Keeping of the society flame. I am, for example, the ranking instructor of debutantes for the cotillion."

"The what?"

"It's a coming-out ball for young society ladies of Baltimore. We always hold it in the magnificent Grand Ballroom at the former Belvedere Hotel. Have you even stayed at the Belvedere?"

"Can't say that I have."

"It was the premiere hotel of Baltimore. A favorite haunt of F. Scott Fitzgerald, you know," she said, as if she and Fitzgerald had been in the same social circles. Never mind the fact that Fitzgerald had died before she was born. "I have also been a leading patron of the Hunt Cup."

"Again, I plead ignorance."

"It's the great, traditional steeplechase of Maryland. Another major society event. A steeplechase is a countryside horse race, in case you are unaware. Our family always had a horse in the Hunt Cup. Won it at least half a dozen times."

But not for many, many years, Arkin thought. It never ceased to amaze him that people of Lily's age could still be so insecure as to feel compelled to assume a haughty manner. To put on airs. He found it mildly irritating. But sad more than anything else. Then he wondered what else Lily did to fill her time. Probably painted atrocious watercolors—like the rose on the wall—that her paltry handful of remaining acquaintances pretended to be impressed with.

"Our records indicate that Father Bryant had nine siblings," he said, beginning to steer the conversation.

"Yes. I'm the youngest. Which is another way of saying that I was the most ignored. My father didn't even attend my birth. By the time I came around, the birth of a child was old hat."

"So, you live here alone?"

"Yes. What of it? There are only five of us still living. My remaining brothers and sisters have established families in other parts of the country. None were interested in moving back into this house."

"Your childhood home."

"That's correct. Collin grew up here too."

"Were you close?"

"Collin and I? We grew to be very close in adulthood, despite our vastly different existential philosophies early on."

"I understand he made waves as a young man, winning a Maryland essay contest with a story about the poor treatment of African Americans by the Baltimore Police Department."

"Collin always was a crusader. Always looking to be a part of something that was bigger than he was."

A door slammed somewhere in the house. Probably Ms. Howard leaving.

"Well, getting down to brass tacks, the first thing I'm interested in is what drew your brother to the Jesuit order."

"The better question is what *drove* him to it. The fear of death, if you ask me. He was traumatized by the death of our older sister, Mary. They were very close. She died when he was quite young. After that, he became a seeker of answers, as I suppose we all are on some level, if we aren't dense or yellow. But Collin ached for reassurance. For adamantine certainties. For a promise, however false, that death would not be the end of him. All of that sort of tripe."

"I take it you didn't share his faith."

"That's putting it mildly. I've been an atheist since high school. The black sheep of the big Catholic family. I did my best to talk him out of going to seminary."

"Did your brother feel he was making a difference in Royburg, the

Kentucky town where he started his parish?" Arkin asked, pretending to take notes on his pad as their discussion wore on.

"Initially, I believe he derived some sort of satisfaction from the fact that he was spreading his beliefs, and that others were comforted by them."

"Initially?"

She smiled a devilish smile. "I'd like to think he was beginning to see the logic of my view of things as time went by."

"Of atheism?"

"Call it what you want. I'd like to think I influenced him over time. That my logical, reasoned outlook rubbed off on him. How could it not? That, and living in that dirt-poor town of forgotten and forsaken negroes. I'm sure it evolved Collin's outlook."

"Did the industrial accident in Royburg further exacerbate things for him?"

"Meaning what?"

"Having so many of his parishioners die on him, young and old alike? Do you think he had a crisis of faith?"

"A crisis of faith," she repeated, sounding almost amused at the question. "He wasn't happy with his God, I can tell you that. We spoke on the phone many times in the wake of the disaster. He asked the usual questions. What God would do this to his followers? What worthwhile lessons could possibly be learned? What was the point of such pain and suffering? He was especially distraught over the wretched and agonizing death of a young boy with whom he'd grown close."

"How did you comfort him?"

"I didn't. I told him that fear of death is for the weak-minded. That's why humanity invented religions. So that the weak-minded could quell their fear of death with fantasies of an afterlife. Why else have religions? One could just go to a decent charm school for the rest of it. No offense."

"Well," Arkin said, doing his best startled Jesuit impression. "I suppose we each have our own ideas about such things."

"I also told him, for the thousandth time, that religions did nothing more than serve as another excuse and basis for extremism and all the violence and horrors that go with it." She paused. "What does this have to do with your research into the long-term impact of Jesuit parishes?"

"I'm also looking at the psychological effect, on the priests themselves, of being immersed in these poor communities. Learning, among other things, whether the difficult conditions caused any of them to question their calling. To question the Faith."

"I see. Well, I don't think he was below questioning his faith toward the end." She paused. To Arkin, it looked almost as if she was struggling to suppress a smile. "But who can ever say what really goes on in another person's mind?"

"Do you think Father Bryant suffered from depression in the wake of the Royburg disaster?"

"Certainly. Who wouldn't be saddened by the curtain being lifted to reveal the falseness of something they'd clung to?"

"Was it your impression that he was perhaps closing in on making a major change with respect to his adherence to the Faith?"

"Who knows?"

"Well, you do, if anyone does. Who was he closer to than you?"

"The only person who really knew what Collin was thinking was Collin."

"Do you think there's any merit to the rumors that Father Bryant killed himself?"

"No," she said quickly. "He had a driving sense of purpose that would have dwarfed any feelings of futility or depression."

"What was his purpose?"

She took a breath. "To make the world a better place, I suppose."

"How so? By what means?"

She shrugged. "His ideas were in constant evolution."

Arkin considered her vague answer for a moment. "What do you think happened? I mean, he was a relatively young man when he drowned. In good health and so forth."

She paused again, still bearing a mystifyingly amused expression. "Well, who can say?" she said at last. "Perhaps he had a congenital heart defect or a brain aneurysm. Those can drop you at any age. Perhaps he slipped and bumped his head and fell overboard. Perhaps he went for a swim and a submerged tree branch caught his pant leg so that the current pulled him under. What does it matter?" she asked in a very matter-of-fact tone.

"It must have been hard on you and your family when he disappeared. Hard to find closure."

"It was a long time ago," she said with a shrug. And again, Arkin had the impression that she was suppressing, of all the incongruous and inappropriate things, a grin.

"Still, those sorts of traumas seem to stay near the forefront of one's memories," Arkin said, in a tone of half appeal, half feigned perplexity.

"My lack of emotion surprises you."

"Well, as you said, it was a long time ago."

"I don't fear death. I don't look at it as an enemy. It's just an endless sleep. Who doesn't like to sleep? If more people looked at it the way I do, there'd be a lot less suffering in the world. A lot less evil perpetrated by fanatics."

To Arkin's ears, she was sounding an awful lot like Sheffield.

"Did you know that your brother's parish was essentially abandoned a few years after his death? Royburg became a ghost town, more or less. For all his work there, all his suffering and heartbreak, the community all but disappeared."

"I wasn't aware."

"No. I doubt such things are mentioned in society newspapers." Arkin capped his pen and stood to leave. "Just out of curiosity, for my own interests, can I ask you, if you don't believe in an afterlife, do thoughts of oblivion really not sometimes keep you awake at night?"

"To allow yourself—"

"I mean, I look around and see the fading vestiges of a once great family. Everything disintegrating around you. And I figure that before long, maybe as soon as 20 years from now, there won't be anyone left alive who ever knew who you or your family were. You'll be forgotten. All your achievements. Your reputation. Your cotillion debutantes and your steeplechase wins. This doesn't sometimes leave you feeling a bit empty? A bit afraid?"

She sat silent for a moment. "I've offended you."

"But not in the way you might think. In my youth, it was people like you . . . ." He stopped himself. "Thank you for your time. I'll see myself out."

*****

That evening, after retrieving his dirty thrift store clothes from the Columbia Island Marina, Arkin found a homeless shelter a stone's throw from the U.S. Capitol Building, where he pretended to be mute and half incoherent and signed in as Jim Seers in order to procure a place to sleep while maintaining anonymity. Still, he worried about whether his cover look was convincing enough. After all, his teeth were straight, and they were all in his head. The whites of his eyes were white, not yellow and bloodshot. His skin looked healthy and taught, not loose, leathery, and rough like everyone else's. And his body odor wasn't about to burn anyone's eyes. Regardless, he was committed. What choice did he have, aside from risking arrest by trying to sleep somewhere out in the cold, maybe in a thicket of bushes in Rock Creek Park or on Theodore Roosevelt Island? Convincing or not, he was staying put.

THIRTEEN

Just as rush hour began the next morning, wearing a baseball cap pulled low, pretending to read a free copy of an alternative weekly paper, Arkin sat on a stoop two doors down and across Swann Street from Trlajic's residence , doing his best to look like a commuter waiting for his carpool pickup. He'd already reconnoitered the alleyway behind Trlajic's home, observing that the man had a dark green Volvo station wagon, and thinking that if he needed to pursue and surveil the man by car, he'd be easy to follow in such a sluggish and clumsy vehicle. He also noted that Trlajic's rear door and two first-floor windows did not have metal security bars over them as did the windows and doors of several other houses in the alley.

Arkin was reasonably sure Trlajic would come out his front door and walk to a bus stop or subway station—that he wouldn't go out his back door and take his car—given that there were so few parking spaces near the U.S. Department of Justice building where DCI's headquarters was located. He didn't have to wait long. A few minutes after eight, Trlajic appeared in the open doorway of his Queen Anne style row house. He was a tall but slouching man in a charcoal gray topcoat and carrying a worn leather satchel-style messenger bag. Arkin was able to ID him from a DMV photo Morrison had texted to him last night. As Morrison would have been entertained to see, the man had a tall, thick head of Balkan hair, as well as big, bushy eyebrows. He turned right after descending his stairs and made his way over to New Hampshire Avenue, where he again turned right, heading toward Dupont Circle. Arkin followed at a discreet distance, assuming the worst—that Trlajic was part of the Priest's group, that he was trained in counter-surveillance techniques, and that he knew what Arkin looked like.

However, within minutes, Arkin's impression was that the man either had no espionage training, or that he considered himself on territory that was so safe that he could let his guard down. He wore headphones and kept his gaze set on the ground in front of him, never seeming to look up, behind, or to either side of him. In short, he seemed oblivious to the world around him. Of course, it was always possible he was playing dumb.

Arkin passed several smallish embassies as he followed Trlajic deeper into the capital. Belarus, Nicaragua, Grenada, Swaziland, Namibia, Argentina, and Jamaica, among others. Approaching what must have been a preschool, Arkin watched Trlajic circumnavigate a group of parents and toddlers gathered at the front steps of a brownstone row house where they largely blocked the sidewalk. As Arkin got closer to the group, he saw, to his horror, a yellow plastic ball about the size of a navel orange roll out into the middle of busy New Hampshire Avenue, with its speeding taxis, buses, and other vehicles. He raced forward, and as he neared the group, he saw what he hoped he wouldn't see. A small boy, maybe 3 years old, toddling toward his ball. The father was fiddling with his smartphone along with half the other adults in the group, oblivious. Without a thought for the risks of Traljic noticing him—the risk of his whole mission being blown—Arkin raced to intercept the child, waving his hands in the air to get the attention of drivers. Traffic slowed and horns blared from the cars of impatient drivers. But Trlajic didn't bother to turn around to see what all the hubbub was about. Arkin was able to scoop up the child and return him to his father who, instead of saying thank you, merely nodded and looked at him with suspicion.

Finally, upon reaching Dupont Circle, Trlajic turned north and went into a Starbucks coffee shop at the corner of 19th Street and Connecticut Avenue. Arkin found a place to observe in the shadow of a building just across 19th Street. Trlajic ordered a coffee, then sat down at a window table and opened a laptop computer he drew from his leather bag. Arkin noted that Traljic sat with his back to the door, in a place with limited exits—not a position a trained intelligence operative would choose. Arkin crossed the street and came up behind

Traljic for a closer look through the window. Trlajic was logging onto Starbuck's free Wi-Fi service and reading the online version of *The Washington Post* newspaper.

Nearly 20 minutes later, Trlajic emerged from Starbucks, crossed the street, and, as Arkin expected, descended the nearly 200-foot-long broken escalator of the Dupont Circle Metro station. Arkin continued to follow as Trlajic caught the Red Line subway, rode it to Metro Center Station, then emerged on surface streets and walked a few blocks to the Pennsylvania Avenue entrance of the U.S. Department of Justice Headquarters Building.

*****

Arkin spent the rest of the day casing Tom Killick's Federal Style red brick condo building on Capitol Hill, figuring out what time of day residents tended to depart and return, memorizing their faces, finding a good spot from which to observe the approaches, and so forth. As darkness fell, he once again retrieved his secondhand clothes from Columbia Island and made his way back to the homeless shelter for the night.

*****

Arkin followed the same schedule the next day. Again, Trlajic stopped to read *The Washington Post* online edition and drink coffee at the Dupont Circle Starbucks before taking the metro to work. The residents of Killick's Capitol Hill condo building came and went at roughly the same times as the previous day. Again, Arkin retreated to the homeless shelter after dark for an anonymous night's sleep.

FOURTEEN

"The eagle has landed," Morrison said to Arkin over the phone.

"Where are you?"

"Already checked into the Crystal City Sheraton. Got a double bed here with your name on it. I'll even let you use my bathroom. For 50 cents."

"Hallelujah."

*****

An hour later, in his regular clothes, Arkin strode through the door of Morrison's room, walked straight to the remaining made bed, and fell face-first onto it.

"Holy cats, this bed feels good."

"Living your cover becoming a bit much for you at your advanced age?" Morrison said.

"I've slept in tents, on airplanes, and in a homeless shelter every night for the past two-and-a-half weeks. Trust me, if I died right here, I'd be happy."

"You're getting soft, Nate."

"If you'll give me just 10 minutes of quiet, to lie here in a tranquility untainted by unintelligible mumbling, Tourette's Syndrome shouts of profanity, or the smells of moldy armpit, fortified wine sweats, or dried urine, I'll be reborn."

"You're being insensitive to the plight of the homeless."

"I'm too tired to care."

"Well, I can't make any promises about the dried urine smell."

*****

Arkin woke to Morrison talking on his phone behind the closed door of the bathroom. Hearing only half of the conversation, Arkin couldn't piece together what it was about. Morrison mumbled on. "The AUSA who ran the grand jury." Pause. "I don't remember. It was three months ago." Pause. "Well, look, I already told what's-his-face that I'm no good with names." Pause. "Then he should have given me a pen so I could write it down. Give me a break," Morrison said, a little louder. "Fine. Talk to you tomorrow."

Morrison emerged from the bathroom looking irritated. "Good morning, sunshine."

"Everything alright?"

"Yeah. Work stuff. Dealing with a pushy little bootlicker at headquarters. Trying to throw me under the bus for his own screw-up. When I still worked in D.C., he's one of a handful of people I told I had an identical twin brother so that when I ran into him in public, I didn't have to talk to him."

"Sounds like an ass."

"A climber. But he'll get his someday. After all," Morrison said, straightening his back and putting on an expression of facetious, exaggerated authority, "ambition sows the seeds of misery."

"Ambition sows the seeds of misery?" Arkin said, a smile spreading across his face. "Did you just come up with that?"

"I'd like to think so. But I probably just heard it somewhere and stored it in my tortured long-term memory."

"Well, it's genius either way," Arkin said, taking a seat at the hotel room's small desk, sipping a cold beer Morrison had just poured for him.

"So, tell me about Lily Bryant."

"She was a piece of work. An angry old atheist who felt alienated and marginalized by most of her uber-rich family, yet was clinging to remnants of the family's social status as if they were the only things keeping her afloat."

"I figured you were wasting your time."

"I wouldn't jump to that conclusion just yet."

"Don't tease me," Morrison said, grinning.

"It seems that back in the day, she was in the process of drawing Father Bryant away from the Catholic faith, planting dangerous ideas in his head about fundamental flaws of the world's religions. She regurgitated the usual Marxist lines."

"So?"

"She also said—wait for it—that religion does nothing more than serve as an excuse and basis for extremism and all the violence and horror that goes with it."

"Sounds like something Sheffield's group might say."

"It does indeed. Plus, she was just a hair too callous discussing the tragic loss of her beloved brother, and a hair too sure that he hadn't killed himself. It could have been my imagination. But I had the distinct impression that she was holding back."

"Holding back what?"

"That Bryant was on the verge of a philosophical transformation shortly before he disappeared. That she knew he didn't drown in the Mississippi River in 1974."

"You're telling me you think she knew he was a fledgling fanatic? That he embezzled money from the parish, staged his own death, and made a run for it to Canada?"

"The only thing I can say definitively is that I had that proverbial funny feeling."

"It doesn't mean Bryant is still alive."

"No, I tend to think that he died many years ago. But perhaps he really did create the group, or at least have a significant role in its founding. That seems more plausible to me than the group merely picking up and exploiting his identity after he died."

"What does that get us?"

"I'm not sure."

They sat thinking for a quiet moment.

"So where are we with our new Serb, Trlajic?" Morrison asked at last.

"My first impression of him is that he has no training whatsoever. Walking down the street, he's as oblivious as Mr. Magoo, wearing headphones, staring at the pavement. He never once tried any of the usual tricks to check whether he was being followed. And most damning, in enclosed spaces, he sits with his back to the entrances and seems to have no concern whatsoever for potential escape routes."

"Could just be that he thinks he's on friendly territory and doesn't need to worry about any of that stuff."

"Possibly. But you know as well as I do that you can never completely switch off the worry about *that stuff,* as you call it, even if you think you're in quote-unquote friendly territory. Any half-decent counter-surveillance training inks the worry habit onto your frontal lobe like a cheap tattoo. Ugly and permanent."

"True. But, like I said, he could just be a non-operative functionary of the group. If he *is* involved, maybe he's not a pair of boots on the ground guy, so to speak, but a pair of soft hands on a keyboard in a cubicle guy. Or maybe he's playing possum."

"Whatever the case, it would be irresponsible of us not to take a closer look."

"What do you want to do?"

"Burgle his house. Take a look at his email. Did you bring your coconut?"

"I did bring my coconut."

The coconut was one of the newer gadgets in Morrison's ATF law enforcement arsenal. It was a small device concealed in a brown coconut-like plastic shell that could create a rogue Wi-Fi hotspot—a hotspot that could be made to imitate a free Wi-Fi hotspot a person uses to log onto the internet every day. Such as the Wi-Fi hotspot at the Dupont Circle Starbucks. If Trlajic logged into his email, bank, or other accounts while inadvertently using Morrison's rogue hotspot, Morrison and Arkin would be able to see everything he did, and gather any passwords he typed in for their own purposes.

Morrison grabbed them another couple of beers from the mini-fridge.

"So what's new in Durango?" Arkin asked.

"Oh, Nate. We have to get you exonerated so you can get back to work. I went on the *best* JTTF raid last week."

"Do tell."

"Do you know my boy Philip Daniels? Deputy U.S. Marshall in the Salt Lake City field office?"

"Don't think so."

"Apparently Daniels has been working undercover, setting himself up as an antigovernment activist on some dirt farm over near La Sal. Putting out subtle bait on internet chat rooms and all that about how he knows people who can get hold of contraband weaponry, explosive components, and all the usual toys. About how he's a former Green

Beret—which is actually true—who can teach fellow patriots all sorts of good combat tricks. Long story short, didn't take long for him to hook some gang of knuckleheads who drove all the way down from Oregon for a promised load of Tovex water-gel explosive. Called themselves the Constitutional Patriot Shock Force."

"Love the name. What was their beef?"

"I don't think they could ever narrow it down. The government is evil. Gun control is evil. Muslims are evil. LGBT people are evil. The Girl Scouts are evil. Sesame Street is evil. The guys were the usual. Bunch of tubby meatheads who got bullied on the playground and couldn't get dates in high school. Made themselves a cool shoulder patch to sew onto the black BDUs they paid too much for at some army surplus store. Probably had a secret handshake."

"So anyway, half the arrest team is hanging out in the basement of the little rambler Daniels has been living in while undercover, watching multiple camera feeds and listening to the transaction unfold via a parabolic Bluetooth microphone we have disguised as part of a meat smoker that Daniels is honest-to-God smoking a pork butt in while we wait so that he can share it with us after the arrest. So, after the Constitutional Patriot Shock Force loads their fake Tovex into their supercool Dodge Grand Caravan minivan, Daniels asks them if they want a few free lessons in practical combat tactics before they hit the road back to Oregon. They say *sure*. He takes them back over to the barn where he stored the fake Tovex and proceeds to teach them a couple of basic things. How to break out of a chokehold. How to target the common peroneal and suprascapular nerve bundle strike points. Then he says, 'Hey, do y'all want to know how to break out of a riot control daisy chain?'"

"What the hell is a riot control daisy chain?"

"Exactly. Daniels made it up. He tells them it's a technique police use for quickly immobilizing large groups in protest or riot situations. A good thing to know how to get out of in the coming struggle against the federal government. *Shit yeah,* they say. *Teach us.* He gets the whole group of them sitting together in a circle with their backs to the middle, then proceeds to zip-tie their hands together behind their backs, and also to each other. So now they're a big cluster of six idiots, literally attached to one another, sitting flat on their asses, each facing a different direction. Needless to say, at that point Daniels spoke the go-for-arrest code word, and we all swept in in full tactical gear to find these poor dopes sitting in a circle on the floor of the barn, looking utterly dumbfounded, already gift-wrapped for us neat as can be. You should have seen their faces. I haven't laughed that hard in years. Laughed so hard I had to sit down. You would have died."

"Sorry I missed it. How was the smoked pork butt?"

"Five stars. It was Daniels' granddad's recipe. His family's from Tennessee. Seems they know how to smoke a hog down there. Anyway, the Marshalls rolled up the whole group. Conspiracy to bomb the Federal Courthouse in Portland, *et cetera, et cetera*. I sent Daniels a case of Gentleman Jack Tennessee whiskey as a thank-you for the barbeque and the laugh."

Morrison's smile faded.

"What?" Arkin asked him.

"Those guys. The Constitutional Patriot Shock Force. They were just so dumb and lost and scared."

"Most of the folks who join those groups are. What was it that Yoda said to the young Darth Vader? *Fear leads to anger. Anger leads to hate. Hate leads to*…domestic terrorism. Or something like that"

"It's like they'd all had fetal alcohol syndrome as kids or something. Not many prospects for them in our modern, fast-paced world. I almost found myself wishing there was some place they could go where they could turn back the clock to a slower, simpler time—where they wouldn't get all anxious and turn into extremist crazies. Almost felt sorry for them."

"You'd have felt even more sorry for all the innocent people they wanted to blow up."

"True. You know something else?"

"What?"

"During the arrest, I remember thinking that this was exactly the type of group Sheffield and his people would have decapitated. Yet here we are, fighting the Priest's group too."

"It's a confusing world."

"Yes, it is."

FIFTEEN

That evening, they visited the Dupont Circle Starbucks that Trlajic favored for his morning coffee and internet browsing.

"What does a coffee snob like you feel like this evening?" Morrison asked as they stood in line. "It's on me."

"Single-origin Timor Mount Ramelau. Clover brewed. Venti." Morrison almost started laughing. "What?"

"Single-origin Timor—"

"Let's have you order that yourself, shall we? I have my reputation as a man to consider." Morrison ordered first. "Do you accept Colorado money?" he asked the cashier.

"I can ask my supervisor," the young man said, utterly serious.

For a split second, Morrison stood there staggered. "That's okay. I'll just use dollars."

Once they had placed their orders, they shifted over to the pickup area where Morrison immediately started making small-talk with the young female barista. "Did you get that in Hawaii?" Morrison said, gesturing to the barista's puka shell bracelet.

She smiled and shook her head. "Tulum."

"Mexico?"

"Yes."

"I've heard good things."

"It's beautiful. You should go."

"If I can ever get time off work."

"I know, right?"

"Do you get decent time off here for vacations and stuff?"

"Oh, yeah. It's a pretty good gig, Starbucks. And the manager is nice. Flexible."

"Speaking of the manager, is he or she here right now? I'm actually supposed to be assessing your electrical system for updating."

"You just missed her. She usually works from 10 to 6."

Morrison was somewhat relieved to learn that he wouldn't have to deal with the manager. "Is she here 10 to 6 tomorrow too?"

"I think so."

"Thanks. I'll come back then. Could I get her name from you?"

"Jessica Stapleton."

"I appreciate it."

SIXTEEN

The next morning, having sanitized themselves of all possible forms of I.D., and shortly before the time at which Trlajic routinely stopped in, Arkin and Morrison sat at a table by the window on the second floor of the Dupont Circle Starbucks—Morrison drinking a basic drip coffee, Arkin drinking something Morrison didn't want to try to pronounce. Arkin had the coconut hooked up to a cheap new laptop Morrison had brought along. It was set up to mimic the Starbucks free Wi-Fi signal and capture the activity of anyone who logged onto it as soon as Arkin activated it. In the meantime, Arkin's eyes were locked on the corner of 19th Street and New Hampshire Avenue, watching for Trlajic. Within 60 seconds of when Arkin predicted he'd arrive, Trlajic appeared. He stood on the corner, waiting for the crossing signal to turn.

"There he is," Arkin said. "You're on."

"Wish me luck."

With that, Morrison went downstairs and explained to a cashier that the manager, Jessica Stapleton, had asked him to inspect the electrical panel for a potential circuit breaker update for a Wi-Fi expansion. The cashier bought his story and led Morrison back to the panel.

"Do you know which breaker controls the Wi-Fi?" he asked. The cashier did not, but got an assistant manager who did. Morrison took notes on the electrical panel brand, the amperage of the different breakers, and so forth, trying to make his visit look legitimate. He turned and looked back across the store to see Trlajic just sitting down at a table and powering up his own laptop. Then Morrison got out his phone and called Arkin, still upstairs and waiting to activate the coconut. "Ready?"

"Ready."

"Here we go." Morrison switched the Wi-Fi circuit breaker off just as Arkin turned on the coconut's rogue Wi-Fi signal—to which they'd assigned the name "Starbucks Free Wi-Fi 2," hoping Trlajic wouldn't notice or care that the usual Starbucks home screen didn't pop up when he opened his web browser. Morrison loitered for another few moments, continuing his fake inspection of the panel, then switched the circuit breaker back on, knowing it would take a couple of minutes for the authentic Starbucks free Wi-Fi router to reactivate itself and produce a signal—by which time Trlajic, happy and oblivious, should already be logged onto the coconut's rogue WiFi signal instead.

*****

"Well?" Morrison asked, back on the second floor with Arkin. Trlajic had just departed after half an hour of internet use.

"Got his personal email account. And Facebook and Instagram."

"Ah, social media. The opiate of the people."

"No banks or anything quite that juicy."

"It's   a   start."

They spent the next couple of hours snooping through Trlajic's email and social media pages. Among other things, they learned that Trlajic's favorite movie was *The Good, The Bad, and The Ugly*, that he liked to post tiresome right-wing rants about liberal politicians, and that he didn't have many friends. They found nothing that suggested Trlajic had any connection to Sheffield or the Priest's group.

"Frustrating," Arkin said.

"He probably has other email accounts."

"Yes, but does he ever log onto them here? And even if he does, how long will it be before he does? And how many times can you pull your fake electrical panel inspection so we can set up the coconut?"

"So what now?" Morrison asked.

"We break into his house."

"Let's do it now, while he's at work."

"No."

"No?"

"We don't know that he's at work. He could be on his way to the dentist."

"He'll go to work after the dentist."

"Don't be rash. Maybe he's getting a root canal and will want to go home afterward to ice his jaw and dope himself up on pain meds."

"Okay. So we do it when he goes to work on Monday, after we track him from his house."

"The Department of Justice Headquarters building has too many exits for one person to cover. He could slip out a side entrance unseen and come home to catch me *in flagrante,* turning his place inside out."

"What's your plan then, smart guy?"

"Tomorrow is Saturday. You'll tail him whenever he goes out while I stay and search his place. That way, you can give me a heads-up whenever he turns for home."

"Won't there be a greater chance of neighbors being home and noticing us on a Saturday? You'd probably have a lot more time in his house if you went in right after he left for work. That's the better plan."

"I *could* do it your way. But then we'd both be wrong."

"It's a stupid plan."

"Thanks for your input."

SEVENTEEN

The next morning, Arkin and Morrison sat in a nondescript rental car at the end of the alley behind Trlajic's house.

"This is boring," Morrison said.

"Complaining is viral misery."

"That's good. A Nate Arkin original saying?"

"Julian Treasure. A business communications guru."

"Well, good for him. I need to take a piss."

"Go behind some garbage cans or something."

"Too many windows looking down on this alley. I can't be getting myself arrested for public urination. Then again, my boss, raging alcoholic that he is, probably has a long rap sheet for that very offense."

Another half hour went by with Morrison holding his urine.

"There's something that's been nagging at me about the idea of Sheffield's group," Morrison said.

"What would that be?"

"Why the extremism? For that matter, why 9/11? Why the Holocaust?"

"Are you dancing around the hard-to-swallow truth that none of us are born evil? That we're all cute and sweet as babies? Are you asking why the Hitlers and bin Ladens of the world go off the rails?"

"Not at all. I already know it's all about existential fear, a love-deprived childhood, self-esteem issues, undescended testicles, *et cetera, et cetera*. What I'm wondering is why all these jerks can't just make due with some nice positive self-affirmations."

"You mean like saying 'I like myself' over and over again in the mirror each morning?"

Morrison smiled. "Well, something like that. I mean, we're all afraid of the same things, right? So why do some of us opt for group therapy, while others of us turn into paranoid, murderous despots?"

"Maybe therapists need to have better advertising."

Morrison chuckled. "Yes. They're missing out on that niche Hitler/bin Laden demographic. If they just had a Don Draper type to—"

"There he is," Arkin said, watching Trlajic emerge from his back door and walk down the steps to the carport where his Volvo station wagon waited. "Keep in touch," he said as he jumped out, and hid behind a parked van.

Morrison followed Trlajic's Volvo down the alley and onto 18th Street, heading north through the Adams-Morgan neighborhood. Trlajic didn't go far. Barely 14 blocks from home, he pulled to the curb on Columbia Road, so Morrison pulled into a no-parking zone a few cars back to watch. Trlajic got out and paid the one=hour limited parking meter. He was carrying a small duffel bag. Trlajic walked passed Morrison's car, before turning into a yoga studio. Morrison got out and walked down the sidewalk, scanning the reception room of the yoga studio as he passed it. No sign of Trlajic. He was probably in a locker room suiting up. Morrison went back to his car, found a better place to park on the far side of the street, half a block away, but where he could keep an eye on Trlajic's car. Then, from under his seat he took a small aerosol can of quick-hardening, gap-filling insulation foam he'd purchased at a hardware store the previous evening, fitted the straw applicator to the nozzle, and tucked it in his coat. He got out of the car, crossed Columbia Road, and made his way down the sidewalk toward Trlajic's Volvo, scanning the street for pedestrians. Reaching Trlajic's car, satisfied that the coast was clear, he crouched down, inserted the straw applicator as deep as it could go into Trlajic's tailpipe, and depressed the aerosol nozzle, filling the tailpipe with insulation foam. It would harden in moments, completely blocking the flow of exhaust and thereby incapacitating Trlajic's car.

"You have the green light for burglary," he told Arkin over the phone after getting back to his rental car.

"He just took his duffel into a yoga studio on Columbia Road."

"Yoga?"

"I know, right? There's something about the image of a big, hairy, bushy-eyebrowed Serb doing yoga that's just comical, isn't there? Anyway, I have eyes on his Volvo, and he isn't going anywhere."

Morrison was glad that Trlajic had parked where there was a one-hour parking meter. It meant that Trlajic probably wouldn't leave his car and walk home. He'd have to sit there feeding the meter as he waited for a tow truck.

Traljic would eventually find out what the problem with his car was, and would then no doubt wonder why someone had deliberately incapacitated his car. If he was indeed involved with the Priest group, then he'd probably figure that someone was taking a look at him. But by that time, with any luck, Arkin would have found whatever he needed at Trlajic's house.

*****

Back at the rear basement door to Trlajic's house, Arkin slipped on a pair of latex gloves, extracted a set of lock picks from his jacket pocket, and set to work on Trlajic's ancient deadbolt, inserting a tension wrench in the bottom of the keyhole and raking a slender pick back and forth along the pins. In less than five minutes, he'd set the pins and was turning the deadbolt open. He stepped into the dark, dank basement of the house, closed the door quietly behind him, then stood and listened. All was quiet.

*****

Five hours later, Arkin and Morrison met at a pizza parlor on 14th Street. "Well?" Morrison asked as they sat down in a booth in far corner of the restaurant. "Don't leave me in suspense."

"Aside from discovering that Trlajic has a thing for chocolate milk and weird black lacquer furniture, I didn't find a damned thing. Turned the place inside-out. Nothing to do with the Priest's group. No fake passport. No tantalizing wall safe. No philosophy books or pamphlets even remotely touching on any of Sheffield's favorite *causa belli*."

"*Causa belli*?"

"Reasons for his actions. Reasons for the group's existence. Reasons for their little ideological war."

"So where does that leave us?"

"It doesn't guarantee that he isn't part of the group. Maybe the group's members are disciplined enough to keep their email accounts and residences sanitized of anything that could link them to the group. Maybe they're being extra careful because they're all on notice that I'm still on the loose and presumably on the hunt."

"Or maybe I just wrecked the tailpipe and muffler on some poor, innocent schlub's car."

"Maybe."

"I'll ask you again, where does that leave us?"

"Let's break into Killick's condo on Capitol Hill. We know for certain that he's in the group, so we're starting from a better place."

"And after that? I'm not paying for a flight to Chile if you don't have anything more than a fax number you traced to Valparaiso. It could be the fax number for the Valparaiso Kentucky Fried Chicken, for all we know."

"Let's just see what we see."

EIGHTEEN

That evening, they sat in their car a few doors down from the front entrance to Killick's condo building. It was raining.

"I scouted this place to time people's departures and arrivals during the workweek," Arkin said. "Being Saturday, that doesn't help us much. But I still think I'll be able to recognize the residents as they approach."

They sat for several minutes in silence. Arkin's face began to grow dark.

"What's wrong?" Morrison asked.

Arkin took a breath. "Thinking about Hannah."

"Yeah? I imagine it's going to hurt for a long time."

"It isn't pain, exactly. It's like a cold, heavy emptiness. Takes the strength out of my shoulders and arms. Makes me want to just go to bed and stay there."

"Do you buy that malarkey about how it's better to have loved and lost or whatever?"

"'Tis better to have loved and lost than never to have loved at all. Alfred Lord Tennyson."

"That's the one."

"I buy it. I buy into it with every fiber of my being."

Morrison just shook his head.

"How come in all the time I've known you, you've never been in a serious relationship?" Arkin asked.

"It isn't legal to marry your horse."

"Really, now. You don't feel like something is missing from your life?"

"Please. Look what you're going through. You think I want to expose myself to that?"

"I just told you it was worth it."

"Look, love always starts off exciting and delightful. But before long, at best, it ends up as nothing more than a thin, inadequate blanket in a world that keeps getting colder and darker."

Arkin smiled as if he harbored a heartening secret. "You're an ignorant man."

They were quiet for half a minute.

"I used to have this dream," Arkin said.

"Do I really want to hear this?"

"It was a recurring dream I had all through my childhood and young adulthood. I had it as far back as I can remember. The setting and finer details changed from dream to dream. But the thrust of it was always the same."

"Did it by chance involve a lumberjack who liked to put on women's clothing and hang around in bars?"

Arkin turned to Morrison, looking half irritated, half perplexed.

"Monty Python?" Morrison asked. "The Lumber Jack Song? Ring any bells? Never mind."

"Every time I had the dream, I would come upon a crystal-clear pond, creek, river, or lake. Whatever it was, it would be full of huge rainbow trout. Absolutely full of fish. A fisherman's greatest fantasy. So immediately, I'd set to figuring out a way to get fishing, driven by a pure, joyous longing. Yearning to catch one. And yet, every time I had the dream, there was a fundamental problem. If I had a fishing rod, I couldn't find a reel. If I had a reel, I couldn't find any fishing line. If I had line, I couldn't find a hook, lure, or bait. I'd be frantic, running around trying to find what I needed before this unlikely schooling of beautiful fish dispersed or disappeared. An exercise in frustration. And even if it was one of those rare dreams in which I was able to finally get everything I needed together, the moment I got my fishing line in the water, I'd wake up." Arkin closed his eyes as if lost in memory.

Morrison sat waiting for more. "Okay. And your point is?"

Arkin opened his eyes and looked at Morrison. "Once I proposed to Hannah, I never had the dream again."

"Huh," Morrison said, looking genuinely thoughtful.

"And the funniest thing is, back when I had these dreams, I'd never even been fishing. My father never took me. Sheffield taught me when I worked for him at DCI. Took me out to a tributary of the Shenandoah that ran off the Blue Ridge Mountains in Virginia."

A young woman was approaching the building with a bicycle.

"There's one of the residents now," Arkin said. "Go."

Morrison jumped out and walked toward the front door of Killick's building at a pace that would have him arrive there a moment after the woman. She unlocked the door and struggled to keep it open as she rolled her bike in. Morrison grabbed the door and held it for her.

"Oh, thank you."

"Of course," he said as he followed her in. Killick's place was on the third floor. Morrison took the stairs, then was pleased to find that Killick's door was around a short corner of the hallway, out of sight of anyone who wasn't going to his condo. Morrison went to work on the locks with the same set of picks Arkin had used on Trlajic's place earlier. Once in, he called Arkin and hit the buzzer to unlock the building's front door.

*****

It was a typical D.C. bachelor pad. Beige wall-to-wall carpet. Beige walls. Bland, big-box hardware store cabinetry, fixtures, and appliances. The first thing they noticed was the stench of molding fruit and rotting garbage. Arkin found what had probably been a bowl of oranges on the kitchen counter which he dumped into the under-sink garbage can and tied off while Morrison opened windows. Killick had been gone for several weeks—having abruptly disappeared once Arkin and Morrison had flushed Sheffield out of hiding in Oregon. From the look and smell of things, he'd left in a big hurry. There were dirty breakfast dishes in his sink. The decaying carcasses of two starved fish—possibly betas—bobbed along the bottom on each side of a partitioned, algae-slick fish tank. On the floor over in one corner of the living room, they saw a spring chest expander, an ab cruncher, and two 45-pound dumbbells—Killick's meager excuse for a home gym. On the other side of the living room, more black lacquer furniture.

"This guy must have the same decorator as Trlajic," Morrison said.

There was one item on the walls that could almost be considered a piece of art. It was a Patrick Nagel print of a black-haired woman in a brown wrap. It was the type of print Arkin might have expected to find in a 1980s fraternity house bedroom. There were four other framed photographs—two on the wall—two on the black lacquer entertainment center. One of Killick on the stern of a large boat holding up a large swordfish. One of Killick holding his fists high in a triumphant pose next to a sign that said, "Mount Kilimanjaro—Congratulations—you are now at Uhuru Peak, Tanzania—5,895m/19,341ft AMSL." One of Killick, shirtless and sweaty, crossing the finish line of a bike race, again with a fist raised high in the air. One of Killick standing in the middle of a line of beautiful women who looked Native American and were each a head shorter than him.

"How pathetic," Morrison said as they both scanned the photos.

"Needless to say, Killick has self-esteem issues. His father was a hypercritical, emotionally unavailable jerk."

"Well, that's something else you two have in common."

Arkin grabbed the photos of Killick with his giant swordfish, took it into the bathroom, and tossed it in the toilet.

"What did you do that for?" Morrison asked.

"Frank Visco says prepositions aren't words to end sentences with."

Half-oblivious to the joke, Morrison went on. "Let's not lose our composure," he said as he strode into the kitchen and opened the refrigerator door looking for something to drink. "Things just got weird."

"What?" Arkin followed him into the kitchen and peered into the refrigerator. Two of the three shelves were filled, wall-to-wall, with bottles of some sort of nutritional supplement drink called "Thor's Hammer Male Enhancement Formula and Stamina Booster—Double Chocolate Flavor."

"Now we know the secret to Killick's renown," Arkin said.

"Really? Is he a player?"

"Only in his own delusional mind."

They took a quick tour of the rest of the condo. As Morrison opened the door to what they assumed would be Killick's guest bedroom, he said, "Things just got even weirder."

Arkin followed him in to see a large table covered with an extremely detailed Z-scale model train set. Two sets of tracks went in and out of tunnels, roughly circling a picture-perfect miniature of a New England coastal town, complete with buildings, houses, crossing signals, a water tower, trees, cars, pedestrians, a small harbor, moored sailboats, even a tiny dog running on the beach. A tiny sign on the main road into town read "Welcome to Bar Harbor, Maine."

"Killick is a model train geek?" Morrison said. "The director of operations of DCI?"

"We're learning all kinds of interesting things today."

"It's like finding out that the commandant of the Marine Corps is into knitting sweaters for cats."

"But what makes this truly weird is the fact that there are no trains in Bar Harbor. It's on an island," Arkin said, picking up what looked like a mailbox key from the top of a small desk in the corner of the room. "Why don't you go downstairs to check his mail while I get started here?"

Arkin started with the desk, going through each of the three drawers, taking his time given that Killick was long gone and they didn't expect their search to be interrupted. But nothing jumped out at him as being relevant. Pens, pencils, a tiny stapler, chewing gum, postage stamps, paperclips, correction fluid, cable bills, paycheck stubs, medical insurance statements of benefits, instructions for how to use the remote control for his flat-screen television, a local phone number scribbled on a Hooters bar napkin marked with a kiss in a tasteless shade of bright pink lipstick.

"Want me to run down that phone number?" Morrison said as he came up behind him.

"No."

"You sure?"

"I can tell you from long experience that Killick has a taste for trashy women."

"Trashy women who like model trains. Still, a Hooters napkin with a kiss on it? Could just be good espionage tradecraft. Seems like a perfect way to make an important phone number look irrelevant."

"Rest assured, it's just a number for some displaced cracker he tried to pick up."

"Are you ever wrong?"

Arkin pretended to think. "Actually, I thought I was wrong once. But I was wrong."

"Suit yourself. There's nothing worthwhile in his mail. It's literally all junk advertisements and so forth, aside from a cable bill and a postcard reminding him it's time to schedule a tooth cleaning with his dentist."

"Thanks."

"How about I go through his kitchen?"

"That would be helpful," Arkin said, turning his attention to the contents of a short two-level shelving unit standing against the wall perpendicular to the desk. It appeared to contain nothing more than books and bound booklets. Most of the booklets were instruction manuals from law enforcement training courses at the Federal Law Enforcement Training Center in Brunswick, Georgia. The books ran the gamut, from a dictionary to a barbeque cookbook to a guide to fishing the Florida Keys. As he went through them on the desktop, a small red and white paperback caught his eye. It was *The Denial of Death*, by Dr. Ernest Becker. He knew right away that he'd seen it before—in Petrović's creepy art gallery in Vancouver. Right before he got shot. He flipped through it, finding numerous underlined passages just like he'd found in Petrović's copy. Passages concerning how anxiety over the concept of mortality—of death—drives men to evil deeds. His interest piqued, given that he'd now found the same book in the premises of two different members of the Priest's group, Arkin flipped it over to read the back cover. It had won the Pulitzer Prize in 1974. The author had been a professor of cultural anthropology at Simon Fraser, San Francisco State, and the University of California at Berkeley. "A brave work of electrifying intelligence and passion, optimistic and revolutionary, destined to endure," according to *The New York Times* Book Review. "It is hard to over-estimate the importance of this book," said the *Chicago Sun-Times*. Clearly the book had made quite an impression on the Priest's group. Though perhaps not in quite the same positive, philanthropic sense its author and reviewers may have anticipated. Arkin pocketed it for later reading, along with a small sequel by Professor Becker called *Escape from Evil*. He didn't figure that the books would help him find Killick and Sheffield. But they might help him better understand the group and its motives.

At one end of the bottom shelf, Arkin saw a bowl half-full of loose change. Killick probably tossed the change from his pockets in there every now and then until the bowl filled, then took it to one of those change sorting machines often found in grocery stores and traded it out for cash. Just in case anything might be hidden under the coins, Arkin dumped the bowl onto the desktop. As he expected, there was nothing in the bowl but coins. But as he swept them back into the bowl with the edge of his hand, he noticed two that were unusual. They weren't quarters, dimes, nickels, or pennies. One was a small, octagonal, gold-colored coin that had *5 pesos* stamped on one side. The other was larger, circular, and consisted of two different metals— a round center of gold-colored metal fused to a surrounding ring of silver-colored metal. On one side was stamped *500 pesos*, and on the other side, the words *Republica de Chile*.

"Got him," Arkin said, emerging from the spare bedroom.

"What is it?"

"Chilean mon—" He stopped mid-statement, something in one of the framed photographs catching his eye as he entered the living room. It was the picture of Killick standing in the middle of the line of Native American-looking women. Each of the women, dressed in simple black dresses, wore an elaborate silver necklace of some sort, each bearing a large upper and semi-triangular lower plate attached via three chains of flat silver links. Most of them had what looked like a mirror image of birds facing each other etched on the upper plate. However, one of the necklaces bore the feature that had caught Arkin's eye. A design. It was on the woman standing to Killick's left. Etched onto the upper silver plate of her necklace, it was a symbol comprised of paired diamond shapes within larger diamond shapes, enclosed by thick zig-zagging lines. It was the same symbol he had seen on Lily Bryant's rug.

"What did you say?" Morrison asked.

"Chilean money," Arkin muttered, his eyes still transfixed by the photo. "Come look at this."

Morrison came over and joined him in examining the photo. "What of it? Killick has an Indian fetish?"

"Do you have any idea what that symbol is?" Arkin asked, pointing it out.

"Not a clue."

"Any idea what tribe this is?"

"I don't know. Maybe Navajo or Hopi. Zuni. Apache. Something southwestern. Maybe a Mexican tribe."

"Have you ever seen necklaces like these?"

Morrison squinted at looked more closely. "I don't think so.

Why?"

Arkin told him about Lily's rug.

"You think it means that she has some connection to the Priest's group," Morrison said.

"Or at least some knowledge of it."

"Should we go put her on the rack?"

Arkin stood quiet for a moment, thinking. "I don't know. Needless to say, we can't compel her to talk by any legal means."

"Sure we can."

"By any *legal* means."

"Well. Bit of a gray area, that. Anyway, you're already a fugitive. And I'm already an accomplice. Whether or not something is technically legal isn't such a huge concern if you ask me."

"Please."

"If it'd make you feel better, we could run our enhanced interrogation plan by that former attorney general guy—what's his name—John Ashcroft. See if it's kosher."

"And then what? Drop her down a hole? Let her run off and alert Sheffield that two renegade vigilante knuckleheads are following his trail to Chile? Spook the quarry? Flush him a second time, and then have no viable leads that we could use to ever find him again?"

"So now what?"

"Now we go to Valparaiso, Chile," Arkin said, taking a close-up photo of the silver necklace in the picture with Killick and the Native American-looking women. "Can you get the time off?"

"I'm feeling sick again. A medium-term illness coming on. I'm thinking it's malaria or amoebic dysentery. Can you believe it?"

"No. But will your superiors?"

"They love me. Anyway, they'll be doing me a favor if they caught me fibbing and fired me. I'd just go to work as a horse breaker."

NINETEEN

They booked their flights separately, Arkin using his stolen passport and fraudulent credit card. Morrison departed two days ahead, planning—for what it was worth—to scout the old colonial Chilean port city of Valparaiso. To get the lay of the land.

Arkin's smartphone chirped as he sat in a departure lounge at Washington-Dulles International Airport. He had a new email. He opened it to discover that it was from a researcher at the Smithsonian National Museum of the American Indian. The text was comprised of a detailed description of the diamond pattern he'd seen on the silver necklace in Killick's photo and on Lily Bryant's rug. He'd sent the photo he took to Morrison who, in-turn, had tracked down the appropriate expert at the Smithsonian through a friend of a friend. According to the expert, the silver necklace was a trapelacucha—a popular and traditional form of jewelry among the Mapuche. The Mapuche were an indigenous tribe of southwestern Argentina and south-central Chile. Prior to the arrival of Europeans, their vast lands ran from the Aconcagua River—north of the capital city of Santiago—nearly 700 miles south to the Chiloé Archipelago. Another vanished empire.

The expert noted that the trapelacucha necklace in the photograph was unusual in that instead of having the usual twin bird symbol etched into the upper plate, it featured a diamond motif symbol known as a "nge-nge," which was a Mapuche term for "eyes that are windows to the soul."

Arkin sat pondering this new information as passengers gathered for his flight. For one thing, it meant that Lily probably had some sort of connection to or at least knowledge of the Priest's group. But how far did it go, exactly? Had her brother founded the group, moved to Chile, and then sent her the Mapuche rug as a gift at some point before he died? At the very least, then, she'd known that her brother hadn't died on the Mississippi River in 1974, but had instead run off to Canada and then South America. But did her knowledge or involvement go further than that? Should he call off his trip to Chile in order to find out? No. Morrison was already down there. Plus, Arkin *knew* the group had a connection to the Valparaiso fax number. He also knew it was only a matter of time before William Cassady of Seattle realized that someone had stolen his I.D. and alerted the authorities, thereby rendering Arkin's passport and credit card useless. No, he'd go to Chile while he still could. He could always come back at a later date to deal with Lily.

TWENTY

Out of an abundance of caution and hoping to make it difficult for anyone to trace his movements, Arkin took a circuitous route south. He flew from Washington, D.C. to Mexico City. From there, he paid cash for a long-haul bus ticket to the small city of Tapachula, down near the border with Guatemala. There, as he'd hoped, he was able to pay cash for his next flight, and avoid using his Cassady identity altogether, by giving the ticketing agent an extra $20 worth of pesos to issue his ticket to Chile in the name of Hector Juarez. No airline or bus service would have any record of a William Cassady travelling any farther than Mexico City. From Tapachula, he took a regional flight—on a new Bombardier turboprop—to Guatemala City. There, he remained in the terminal to avoid having to go through customs, then caught his continuing flight to Bogota, Columbia, and, at long last, Santiago, Chile.

TWENTY-ONE

"You must pay a fee," the Chilean customs officer said.

"Pardon?" Arkin asked. Mindful of the numerous security cameras, he was wearing a baseball cap low across his forehead, doing his best to keep his face hidden.

"You must pay a fee," she repeated in stiff, sharply annunciated English, as though it were a memorized phrase comprising her entire knowledge of the language.

"A fee?"

The officer, her hair up in a tight bun, sighed in frustration as she pointed to a booth on the far side of the entrance hall that Arkin had passed without noticing, off to the side of the main customs queue. He took deep breaths and blinked his eyes repeatedly as he made his way there, trying to clear his gummed eyes and shake off the fatigue of his restless red-eye flight. Arriving at the proper queue, he asked an American backpack-wielding girl what the fee was about.

"It's a reciprocity fee. It's like a $130."

"Do they take credit cards?"

"I don't know."

Arkin cursed himself for not reading the travel tips sections of the Chile guidebooks he studied in Seattle bookstores while plotting his route south. He was down to $62 in cash, which he'd hoped to use on bus fare to his rendezvous with Morrison. A customs entry fee was such a trivial thing. Yet it could be his undoing. How could he have been so stupid? Plus, he'd now have to use the Cassady credit card, wrecking his efforts to obscure his trail from anyone who might have ready access to credit card data. His arrival in Chile could still be tracked through his use of the Cassady passport. But foreign customs entry data was often a lot harder to get hold of than American credit card data.

"Do you take credit cards?" he asked as he at last reached the counter.

"Si."

The clerk swiped his William Cassady Visa card. Arkin heard a beep. The clerk swiped it again, then waited. And Arkin waited, watching the clerk's eyes. What was happening? Arkin couldn't see the screen of the card reader, but wouldn't have been able to read the Spanish even if he could. Several seconds went by. Was something wrong? The clerk was still focused on the reader, waiting. Then, another beep.

"Sir, the card no, ah, no accept."

Oh, shit. Could the existence of the fraudulent card have been discovered this quickly? Unlikely. Maybe it was just a security policy of the issuing bank to block overseas transactions without prior notice of planned travel from the cardholder. He should have called to tell them he would be travelling abroad. Another silly error with potentially disastrous consequences. But the cause of the decline hardly mattered now. He turned the credit card over to view the customer service number. But it was a futile gesture. He knew perfectly well that his cheap cell phone wouldn't work in South America.

"I don't have cash. Is there a wire transfer—uh, is there a—"

The issue caught him off guard. His tired mind spun. His face felt hot. His heart pounded in his ears. He looked all around as if searching for an escape route.

"Sir?" said the girl with the backpack. "I can loan you the money to pay the difference."

Arkin exhaled. "Bless you. I can call my credit card company from a payphone as soon as we clear customs, and then draw cash from a bank machine to pay you back. And I'll buy you any cocktail you want as a thank you gift."

"Just one? I'm kidding. No worries," she said, smiling as she handed him a wad of cash. "You can get me that Chilean cocktail, the pisco sour."

"You got it."

His reciprocity fee paid, Arkin made his way back to the passport control queue. Standing there, he began to worry anew, wondering if Chilean customs was linked up to RMAL, or any of the other new, post-9/11 international movement alert systems. If they were linked to any of the international systems, the customs officer would only have to scan the passport's barcode, or simply key in the passport number, to access a full set of data on Cassady, along with an enlarged full-color photo. Did he really look enough like Cassady to pull this off? He didn't know.

Then he worried that Cassady might already have discovered that his passport was missing and reported its loss to the State Department. He even worried—though the possibility seemed ridiculously remote—that Cassady himself might be wanted by Interpol. What wretched luck that would be.

"Norteamericano?" the kind-faced customs officer asked as Arkin walked up to his booth.

"Yes. Si."

"Passport, please."

Sure enough, the man scanned the barcode on the back page of Cassady's passport, then looked up at the computer screen that was turned just too far for Arkin to see. The officer furrowed his eyebrows, gave Arkin a glance, then resumed his examination of whatever was on the screen. A few seconds later, he picked up his telephone, pressed a pre-programmed button, and muttered something into the receiver. All Arkin could make out was, "Si, si." He hung up, looked up at Arkin with an obviously forced smile, and said, "Momento, señor."

Arkin stiffened, but didn't panic. After the reciprocity fee scare, his senses were in overdrive, his mind kicked up to a heighted level of function and awareness that he used to call "combat mode" back in the days of his recon and counterintelligence work. In this state of mind, his thoughts seemed to speed up while the world around him slowed down. He was better able to think, to prepare, to act quickly.

Had they somehow figured out that nobody named William Cassady had been on the flight from Bogota? Were they expecting to see a passport in the name of Hector Juarez? He couldn't imagine their customs security was that quick or tight. Then again, anything was possible. Whatever the case, it was obvious there was going to be trouble. Perhaps he didn't look enough like Cassady to fool this official. Perhaps the passport was somehow compromised.

In due course, Arkin saw two uniformed customs officers, each with holstered side-arms, emerge from an unmarked door in a far wall and make a beeline for him. They would probably take him back through the same doorway. He could try to run for it, but the exit to the terminal was still a good distance down a crowded corridor, and there were too many people around who could play good Samaritan and try to trip him up. No—as long as they didn't try to cuff him on the spot, he'd wait for a better opportunity.

"Sir, would you come with me, please?" asked one of them, taking the Cassady passport from the other officer. At a bulky 6-foot, he was the larger of the two who'd come from the unmarked door.

"Is there a problem?"

"Come with me, please, sir."

Arkin wasn't about to push his luck demanding an explanation. If he made a scene, it would give them all the more reason to cuff him. And both officers were carrying what looked like Peerless model P010 handcuffs. He nodded, and followed the larger officer toward the unmarked door, while the second officer followed behind, too close for good escort technique. Passing though the doorway, Arkin was pleased to see a long, dimly-lit, windowless passageway that made a 90-degree turn at its end. As soon as the door closed behind them, Arkin threw a vicious elbow into the trailing officer's nose, dropping him to the ground. The sound of the strike got the big, lead officer turning for a look. But before he could come around to effectively defend himself, Arkin hit the side of the officer's neck with his forearm. The officer fell to the floor, unconscious. Arkin turned to see the trailing officer also unconscious, flat on his back and bloody, but hopefully not fatally injured.

Arkin didn't have time to check the man's condition. He listened for the footfall of anyone alerted by the sounds of his attack, heard nothing, grabbed his apparently compromised passport from the one officer's hand, then tiptoed down the hall to peer around the corner. There were four offices on one side of the hallway, each with windows tinted with what might have been one-way glass treatment. The blinds were drawn in every one of them. Interview rooms, Arkin guessed. Behind the closed door of the first one, he could hear the unintelligible muffle of a hushed conversation. The next two were dark. The fourth was lit, and the door was open, but nobody was inside. It was probably where they'd been planning to take him. He passed the last room, quickly and quietly, before turning another corner into what looked like a locker room and coffee break area. Mercifully, it was vacant too. Arkin grabbed a nondescript brown corduroy jacket and a gray baseball-style hat off a coat rack, put them on after dropping his own jacket and hat in a trash barrel, then popped through the far door and out into the main terminal area, clear of customs.

The air smelled of warm pastries and coffee, driving home the point that he was hungry after his inadequate airline breakfast. But he dared not stop for food. He made his way not to baggage claim, where he might reasonably be expected to go, but to the check-in area, then straight out the nearest door where he grabbed a cab as it disgorged its departing travelers.

"Estación Parajitos, por favor."

"Si."

As they crossed derelict pastureland and entered the outskirts of Santiago, Arkin mimed his need for a payphone and an ATM machine. As soon as the cab driver found a phone, Arkin called the toll-free number of his Cassady credit card. To his considerable surprise, the call went through. To his even greater surprise, after confirming Cassady's ZIP code, as well as the fake mother's maiden name Arkin had put on the credit card application, they apologized for Arkin's inconvenience, set up a four-digit pin for him, and reactivated his card with a note to allow transactions in Chile. After declining to participate in the credit card company's customer satisfaction survey, he walked half a block down the street to an ATM machine where he drew—in Chilean pesos—the full $200 cash advance limit on the Cassady credit card. At the bus station, with impeccable politeness and soft voice, he paid cash for a ticket on the slow local bus to Viña del Mar, with stops in Curacavi, Casablanca, Villa Alemana, Quilpue, Viña del Mar, and Reñaca. Removing his hat and jacket and bundling them on a nearby bench, he then went to a different ticket window, where he played the archetype of the obnoxious, loud, conspicuous American tourist, purchasing a ticket for the sleeper bus crossing the Andes Mountains to Mendoza, Argentina, with the Cassady credit card, feigning confusion, and twice demanding confirmation, por favor, that his ticket was indeed to Mendoza, señor, and not to Maipú.

From the ticket counter, he made a quick study of the schedule board while retrieving his hat and jacket, exited to the bus queuing area, gave his ticket to the driver, and boarded the sleeper bus to Mendoza. He made his way to the very back of the bus before putting his hat and jacket back on. After a moment, he slipped off again while the driver's back was turned as he loaded bags. Arkin walked 30 feet, and then boarded the local bus for Reñaca. In five minutes, they were off.

TWENTY-TWO

Several hours later, Arkin disembarked one stop short of his ticketed destination, in the coastal resort city of Viña del Mar. The cool salty air rolling in off the Pacific was a welcome change from the dry heat of the Chilean interior. The sun had set as they entered the city, and now Arkin could see, across the dark waters of a broad crescent of bay, the thousands of soft glowing amber lights of the old colonial Spanish port city of Valparaíso. Little San Francisco, as it was known to some. The colorful, eclectic, and vibrant birthplace or one-time home to the likes of Pablo Neruda, Salvador Allende, and, more notoriously, Augusto Pinochet—its neighborhoods and winding streets clinging to steep hillsides, perched above the southeastern Pacific Ocean.

Arkin gave himself a moment to breathe, then walked toward the waterfront until he found a corner grocer, where he ducked in and bought himself a razor, a bottle of water, three bananas, and a round loaf of white bread. He devoured the food in a small park around the corner. After that, he ducked into the public restroom and did his best to shave his head with a crude lather made from tap water and the bathroom's heavily perfumed pink hand soap.

Given that it would now be utterly foolish to use the Cassady credit card, Arkin opted to conserve his cash by taking the commuter train, instead of a taxi, from Viña del Mar around the bay to Valparaíso. It was a surprisingly quick ride to the line's terminus at Puerto Station. From there, somewhat disoriented, he walked inland until reaching the Plaza Justicia. There, in front of the old courthouse, he found himself standing in the shadow of a tall statue of Lady

Justice. Yet she was no typical Lady Justice. She wore no blindfold of impartiality. Stranger still, in a seemingly casual and unconcerned manner, she held what appeared to be disassembled scales of justice in a loose jumble at her side. Tarnished and soiled with pigeon droppings, she bore an unmistakably confident expression that Arkin knew full well was nothing more than a brave façade.

Back on course, he skirted the bustling Plaza Sotomayor, and began the long, circuitous climb up into the Cerro Alegre neighborhood. The night air was a mix of strong aromas—roasting coffee beans on one block, baking bread on the next, urine and stale water in the alleys in between. Warm light glowed within old wooden window frames as Arkin climbed the steep, winding streets. The murmurs of distant conversations floated across the night air. He limited his search for cheap lodging to the most bohemian of streets, reasoning that that was where the most low-cost backpacker-oriented options would be found. Before long, he came across a reasonably clean-looking hostel with the smell of frying onions emanating from its kitchen window. Seven dollars per night for a clean bed in a shared room containing four sets of bunks. That was good enough. And as he signed the register as Jeff Leary of Toronto, Ontario, the night manager didn't seem the least bit suspicious of his story that his backpack, containing his passport, had been stolen as he slept on the overnight bus from Mendoza. "Ah, Argentina," the man said, rolling his eyes and tsk-tsking.

Arkin took a shower. It was his first real shower in several days, and he lingered under the warm water, washing himself with discarded fragments of three different soaps left behind by others. Then he washed his clothes in the bathroom sink with the hostel's hand soap, and, wearing nothing more than a threadbare hostel towel, tiptoed down the dim hallway to his room. To his relief, it was still empty, his roommates no doubt out on the town enjoying an evening of good food, wine, and conversation. He hung his clothes on the railing of the bunk bed to dry, then hit the sack. He slept 12 full hours.

TWENTY-THREE

The next day, Arkin woke to a city lit bright by the morning sun. He grabbed a hostel breakfast of day-old baguette with butter and blackberry jam, washed it down with a cup of Earl Grey tea with milk, and then set off to get the lay of the land. The houses and other buildings in the neighborhood surrounding the hostel were a hodgepodge of antiquated architectural styles. Many of the old houses were painted in one of a rainbow of colors—tinted and cobalt blues, canary and lemon yellows, pale greens, pastel purples, pinks. A beautiful shambles of faded grandeur. He wandered the streets, going wherever his curiosity led him.

At the end of one street, he came across the upper station of a rickety old funicular, and across from that, a small corner grocer. He decided to use some of his precious cash to purchase two six-packs of Chilean beer—bait he would later use to draw in an unwitting accomplice to a plan he had to gather information related to the fax number he'd found at the gallery in Vancouver. He took the beer back to the hostel, hid it under his bed, then departed once again, heading for his rendezvous with Morrison.

They'd chosen the rendezvous location and potential meeting times before leaving the U.S., having spotted a promising spot using satellite photos provided by Google. It was a large, old hillside cemetery in a part of the Cerro Panteón neighborhood affording sweeping views of Valparaiso Bay and the open Pacific. It didn't look like much from the outside, its high whitewashed walls marred with graffiti. But upon entering through the massive iron gates and

Romanesque portico of the main entrance, Arkin found himself looking down a grand row of massive stone and marble mausoleums and family sarcophagi. Clearly, this was a cemetery for Valparaiso's rich and elite—not its regular citizens. Many of the grave markers listed dates in the 1800s. Many of the façades were cracked—no doubt from the many powerful earthquakes that had hit Valparaiso over the centuries.

The cemetery was something of a maze, with tall mausoleums and old trees lining numerous spur pathways shooting off from the main avenue of the dead in all directions. Arkin made his way down the main avenue, then turned left at the third spur. Fifty yards down the path, he found Morrison studying a marble sculpture of the Virgin Mary standing atop a short sarcophagus. Its nose was missing, having either fallen or been deliberately broken off.

"Excuse me, sir, but I think we are acquainted," Arkin said.

"You were supposed to be here yesterday," Morrison said with feigned irritation. They'd planned to try for the rendezvous in the same place and time each day until they both made the meeting.

"Sorry. I took the scenic route."

"Whoa! Nice haircut. I hope you got the stylist-in-training discount."

"I didn't leave myself a tip, I'll tell you that."

"How was the trip? Any issues?"

"Oh, well now. Where to begin?"

As they walked the lonely pathways of the cemetery, Arkin filled him in on the story of his trouble at passport control at the airport.

"Yes," Morrison said. "I thought that was you."

"I was in the news?"

"You were. There was a photo of you on the front page of the paper. But it's a black-and–
white security cam still taken from overhead. It's impossible to tell who you are. Especially with that baseball cap pulled low over your eyes. Not to worry. Although I wouldn't use the Cassady passport or credit card again."

"You don't say."

"What's the plan?"

"How many times have you asked me that in the past seven days?"

"Hey, I'm *your* monkey. You ain't mine."

"Whatever that means. Why don't we start with your impressions of the environment?"

"Very good, sir. The local police here—the Carabineros—are very professional, very straight, but underequipped. They carry only Brazilian Taurus .38s. And they're relatively slow to respond to emergency calls, due in no small part to their underpowered cars and the steep terrain and narrow streets around here."

"How do you know their response speed for emergency calls?"

"Don't ask. Let's just say I created a small handful of emergencies, then sat back and studied."

"But nobody knows your face? Nobody is looking for you?"

"Don't insult me. I'm a professional."

"Where are you staying?"

"Little fleabag hotel in the Cerro Allegre neighborhood. You?"

"A hostel in the same neighborhood."

"That'll be convenient."

"Did the guns arrive?"

"The UPS tracking thing says they did. But the hotel keeps guest mail back in the manager's office where I can't see. I didn't think it would be wise to try to break in."

"Shall we go try to retrieve them?"

"Sure."

*****

Before leaving the U.S., Morrison had shipped two compact Sig Sauer P238 pistols inside of two hollowed-out dictionaries packed in a box with other books. The box was addressed to a "Mr. Kronos"– Morrison's idea of a joke related to what he'd started to call Arkin's quest for patricide: his quest to bring down his father figure, Roland Sheffield—care of a random three-star hotel on a quiet, narrow street in the Cerra Bellavista neighborhood. At great expense, he'd shipped the package via overnight mail. At even greater expense, and to help ensure that the hotel would hold onto the mail, he'd made a reservation in the name of Mr. Kronos using a credit card number he had gotten from one of his maternal uncles. His uncle—an ex-convict and diehard libertarian who lived in rural Mississippi—didn't press for details when Morrison told him he didn't want to book the hotel in his own name.

Approaching the hotel from opposite ends of the street, Arkin and

Morrison looked for any sign of surveillance—taking care just in case the guns had been discovered by Chilean customs and a trap had been set to arrest the involved smuggler. They didn't go straight to the hotel. Instead, they each passed by it and then met on the opposite side of the block.

"Did you see anything?" Arkin asked.

"Looked all clear to me. There was a woman standing in the window of a boutique looking at a dress or something. But she didn't give me the surveillance vibe."

"I saw her too. I think she's a civilian."

Arkin walked back around the block to the hotel while Morrison watched his back, trailing him by a couple dozen yards. He entered the cramped lobby—really just a small room with a threadbare couch and tall, skinny table with a pot of complimentary tea sitting on a hotplate. Having heard the bell in the door chime as Arkin entered, a clerk appeared in a small service window.

"Hello," Arkin said. The clerk nodded. "Do you speak English?"

"Yes, of course."

"My name is George Kronos. I don't check in until tomorrow. But I believe you received mail shipped here for me."

"Con permiso," the clerk said, disappearing from the window. He reappeared with the package. "You have passport?"

"It was stolen."

"In Chile?"

"Argentina."

"Ah." He nodded, as if that made perfect sense. Arkin was beginning to think the Chileans didn't hold the Argentinians in terribly high esteem.

"Any identification?"

"I'm afraid not."

The clerk stood still, staring at Arkin as if trying to memorize his face. Or as if he'd seen it somewhere before. On television? In the newspaper? On a police flier? Perhaps Chilean customs had circulated the passport photo of Cassady, and he looked enough like Arkin to earn Arkin second glances from wary clerks in hotels frequented by foreigners.

Not wanting to make the clerk any more suspicious, Arkin suppressed an urge to look over his shoulder, through the glass doorway and into the street, where he half-expected to see a squad of uniformed Carabineros waiting to march him off to prison.

Shit.

At last, the clerk handed the package out through the window. "Until tomorrow then."

"Thank you. See you tomorrow."

TWENTY-FOUR

"So now what?" Morrison asked as they walked toward Morrison's hotel to stash the guns.

"After we drop these off, we strategize."

"Why don't we go strategize over one of those famous grass-fed steaks and a cheap bottle of red," Morrison said.

"There's great red wine here, to be sure. But you're thinking of Argentina for the beef."

"Well, what food are the Chileans famous for then?"

"I don't know. Maybe empanadas de machas."

"What's that?"

"Sort of a Hot Pocket stuffed with surf clams and cheese."

"That sounds good. Let's go. I'm buying. Oh, and here," Morrison said, pulling a Samsung smartphone from his pocket and handing it to Arkin. "Now we both have Chilean cell phones."

"Is it stolen?"

"Do you care?"

Arkin thought for a moment. "No."

*****

They sat in an ancient black-and-white checkerboard tile-floored bistro near the Plaza Mayor that had a long wooden bar that looked at least a century old and ran nearly two-thirds the length of the place. The bistro was long and narrow and had a high ceiling. Behind the bar were innumerable, multi-colored bottles of liquor. Piscos, brandies, classic aperitifs and digestifs like Pernod, Aperol, Campari, Cynar, and others with unfamiliar names, many of them decorated with highly artistic, old-fashioned labels. There were numerous framed black-and-white photos of people in Victorian clothing hanging from the warped plaster walls. Antique light fixtures provided dim light and a standup piano stood against a wall in the rear, silent and dusty. The whole place struck Arkin as something that had been frozen in time for the better part of a century. They could have been sitting in a bistro of 1920s Paris.

Arkin and Morrison sat at a rickety wooden table, devouring excellent grilled salmon, cow tongue in some sort of walnut sauce, heart of palm salad, and French fries that were as big as carrots.

"Alright," Morrison said as their server poured them each a tiny glass of some sort of reddish-brown bitter Chilean digestif called Araucano. "I'll ask you again: what's our next move?"

"Well sir, as you know, my internet searches for the fax number turned up jack squat. In the U.S., of course, it would be easy enough for us to link a fax number to an address. But how do we do that in Chile?"

"Get a voice number for the same business, assuming there is one. Then call and ask what their address is."

"And how do we do that?"

"A lot of times, fax numbers are one digit off from voice numbers."

"True. So, then, what? We start calling numbers that are close to the fax number until we get one that sounds right?"

"You sound skeptical."

"I'm willing to try anything. But neither of us speak much Spanish. Plus, how will you know if and when you hit the right number? You'll get random individuals. Random businesses. Calls without answer. You won't know what's what. Here's another idea."

"Lay it on me."

"I can send a fax to the number. I'll make the header look important, maybe with some counterfeit bank or government letterhead. But then I'll make the rest of the fax blurry and unreadable. Then, hopefully, the header will make them worry that they're missing out on an important fax. They'll send a reply to the originating fax number, hopefully with an address or phone number on it."

"Clever. But you think they'll fall for it? And what fax machine are you going to use?"

"One in a hotel business center or private mailbox or office supply type of shop," Arkin said.

"What if they do a Google search of the fax number? Won't they see that it's from a hotel or mailbox place instead of a bank or government ministry or whatever you're pretending to be? And then won't they smell a rat? And what if the fax number is only used for their assassination missions? Then receiving some random fax might really set off alarm bells."

"That's a risk. But our options are limited."

"Let's try my way first."

TWENTY-FIVE

Using his new smartphone to search, Arkin found a nearby hotel with a business center—and, presumably, a fax machine. It was on the outskirts of the resort city of Vina del Mar, just under four miles to the northeast. They walked down from the restaurant to the waterfront and boarded a light rail train at the Bellavista metro station. As they walked and rode, Morrison dialed numbers that were one or two digits off from the fax number Arkin had found in Vancouver. A few didn't answer. A few were clearly for individuals who merely answered with an "Aló," "Hola," or "Digame." A handful seemed to be for businesses of some sort. One was for a library—Morrison knew the word "biblioteca."

"Maybe we can get someone who speaks Spanish to call these numbers for us," Morrison said.

"Maybe."

They got off the train at Miramar station, walked to the modern monstrosity of a hotel, strode through the main entrance as though they belonged, and found an English language directory next to the elevators that listed the business center as being on the second floor. Minutes later, they were sitting at side-by-side computer terminals. In a few minutes, Morrison was tracking down an image of the blue-and-red seal and coat of arms for the Gobernación Provincial de Valparaíso—the provincial government of Valparaiso. Arkin copied and pasted it onto the top a document he was turning into counterfeit government letterhead.

Morrison used a free language translation website to find the

Spanish equivalent of the phrase, "Notification of immediate action...." It translated to "Aviso de acción inmediata," which they both hoped fit with the local Chilean dialect of Spanish. Then Arkin typed the phrase below the coat of arms of the fake letterhead. On subsequent lines, he typed random letters, filling space. He printed the document, placed it on a copy machine, and just as the copy machine scanner reached the area between the line reading "Aviso de acción inmediata" and the body of the letter, he slid the sheet of paper so that everything below the line that said "Aviso de acción inmediata" was blurred. His first couple of attempts didn't quite work, resulting in either some of the gobbledygook lines of text remaining clear enough to see, or part of the phrase "Aviso de acción inmediata" ending up too blurred to read. On his third try, he nailed it. The letterhead and "immediate action" phrase looked perfect, and everything below was too blurry to make out.

Arkin set the document in the feeder of the business center's fax machine and keyed in the number.

"Cross your fingers," he said to Morrison as he pushed the dial button. The machine beeped to life, emitting the individual tones of numbers as it dialed. The line rang its foreign sounding ring. After three rings, the familiar click of the line being answered. Arkin held his breath as all was silent. Then, to his tremendous relief, he heard the squeaky tone of the answering fax machine. Arkin exhaled. The number still worked. And a few seconds later, the hotel fax machine spit out a confirmation sheet indication that the fax was sent and received successfully.

"So now we wait?" Morrison asked.

"Now we wait. We wait right here by this fax machine."

*****

They sat in soft armchairs in a corner of the business center, next to tall windows that framed panoramic views out over Valparaiso Bay. They had the business center to themselves.

"I've been thinking about your pursuit of Sheffield and the Priest's group in the context of the big picture," Morrison said.

"Big picture?"

"Of your life. Of life in general."

"Oh, no. Is this going to be another rant?"

"You realize you're chasing yourself, right?"

"What?"

"In chasing Sheffield and the phantom Priest, you're chasing versions of yourself. Other fundamentalists."

"I'm a fundamentalist now?"

"In a way. The only real difference between y'all is that that you each stubbornly, stupidly adhere to different codes. And really, your respective codes aren't all that different. Same goal. Just different in the details."

"Such as that I don't murder people?"

"Come on now. You have your cute little law enforcement officer's sort of Bushido code, with your strict adherence to inflexible black and white, good and evil views of people and their behaviors."

"Clearly, I've relaxed my standards of late, what with my stealing someone's I.D., assaulting uniformed law enforcement officers in Canada and Chile, and so forth."

Morrison went on as though he didn't hear him. "And Sheffield has his grandiose scheme-to-save-the-world code. I wonder if you were both driven to it by the same thing."

"To what?"

"To fundamentalism."

"Good lord."

"Probably by that extra-sharp existential anxiety that's so often a product of low self-esteem."

"Extra-sharp? Are you talking about existential anxiety or cheddar cheese?"

"Of course, it's always about anxiety, isn't it? Our biggest psychological issue, as a race."

"Are we having a conversation, or are you just talking to yourself?"

"But then the 99-dollar question is *why* would you and Sheffield and maybe even the Priest—each of you total studs, with resumes that nearly put you on par with the superheroes of Marvel Comics—why would you, of all people, have low self-esteem?" Morrison, suddenly lost in thought, stared out the window toward the sunny Pacific.

"A thought-provoking session, Doctor Morrison. Worth every penny of my co-pay."

"You're just irritated that I'm so accurate in my—"

His statement was interrupted by the hotel fax machine chirping to life once again as it received a call. With agonizing slowness, with Arkin and Morrison hovering over it, staring, willing it to hurry up, the machine rolled out a single faxed page with a hand-written note and phone number on it. Morrison, back at one of the computer terminals, typed the content of the note into the English-Spanish translation web page to reveal that it said, "Fax message received but unreadable. Please resend or call to discuss." The phone number was double-circled. Apparently, they'd prefer a straight-up phone call to another fax.

"Did that really just happen?" Morrison said, staring at the screen.

"You mean, did something finally go our way? Did our little scheme work like a charm? Did the objects of our pursuit just unwittingly and willingly give us their phone number? I don't know. Pinch me."

"How about if I just slap you?"

"Google the phone number."

Morrison did. But nothing came up. No name. No address.

"I guess I spoke too soon," Morrison said.

"You always do."

TWENTY-SIX

Arkin sent Morrison home for the evening, thinking that having the two of them together would be overkill for the next move he had in mind. Then, after a solitary late dinner of cold cheese empanadas and lukewarm black tea back at his hostel, he put the Chilean beers he'd bought earlier in a washtub of ice he'd coaxed out of the hostel manager and set himself up, with the tub of beer at his side, in a worn rocking chair on the hostel's wide back porch overlooking Valparaiso Bay. It was fairly dark on the porch, a single string of multi-colored Christmas lights providing the only illumination. Alone, he cracked open a cold beer, took a long drink, and waited, taking in the sweeping view of the Pacific.

After about 10 minutes, two young men in Peruvian wool sweaters joined him, taking seats on a threadbare couch against the wall. They were having a muted discussion in Spanish as one of them fished a pack of cigarettes from his shirt pocket. Neither of them looked a day over 18, and it occurred to Arkin that his age might make him dangerously conspicuous here. He was a little old to be staying in hostels. Guests might suspect him of being an old peeping pervert or drug dealer of the sort Arkin remembered seeing lurking around the lesser hostels he stayed in while backpacking through Europe as a freshly emancipated 18-year-old.

"Hola," Arkin said, nodding to them.

"Hola."

"Hablas Ingles?"

They shook their heads.

"Cerveza?"

"No, gracias. Cigarillo?" one of them asked, holding the pack out for Arkin.

"No, gracias."

The men lit up. And while Arkin was usually repulsed by cigarette smoke, he found the toasty aroma of whatever brand they were smoking surprisingly pleasant. He leaned back in his comfortable chair, closed his eyes, drew a deep breath through his nostrils, and allowed himself a moment of relative relaxation.

Five minutes later, they were joined by a tall blond man accompanied by two Latin-looking women. They looked to be in their 30s, which Arkin found reassuring. There were holas all around.

"Cerveza?" Arkin offered the newcomers.

"Si!" they said, in unison.

"Hablas Ingles?" he asked again as he handed out their beers.

"Yes," they all said.

"Are you American?" the man asked, his tone not altogether friendly.

"Canadian. You?"

"Dutch," said the man.

"Argentine," said each of the women.

Bingo.

They compared stories of their journeys, with Arkin telling half-truths about how he'd just arrived from Vancouver, with no certain destination in mind, but was very much looking forward to reuniting with an old friend. Before long, his candidates each had several beers in them. They were laughing, discussing favorite movies, philosophizing about the value of an unencumbered singles lifestyle, and complaining about post-9/11 American foreign policy, all as though they'd known each other for years. Arkin even smoked a cigarette one of the women offered, though it made his stomach turn, just to add to his crafted aura of fellowship.

In truth, he found the conversation utterly banal. The women were at least tolerable, and certainly friendly. But after listening to 10 minutes of the arrogant Dutchman's inane and idealistic diatribe on the evil of America, Arkin found himself struggling to subdue visions of sarcastically congratulating the bastard on his countrymen's "great job protecting the innocent civilians of Srebrenica, Bosnia," then jamming his head in a toilet and flushing it. At one point, the

Dutchman even turned his back to Arkin and bent over to help himself to another of Arkin's beers, leaving his scrotal area so totally exposed to attack that Arkin groaned with temptation, passing it off as a groan of satisfaction as he stretched his arms. But he contained himself and kept up the façade.

At long last, the idiot Dutchman ran out of steam. Either that, or he finally realized, too late, that the women were finding him a bore. Whatever the case, he went to bed.

"Are the Argentine and Chilean dialects the same," Arkin asked the two Argentine women, after gently steering the conversation to the topic of regional linguistics by complaining that the Spanish he studied in high school didn't seem to help him a lick this far south.

"Different, in some ways. The accent, also different."

"Hey," Arkin said in as nonchalant a tone as possible, as though a thought has just occurred to him out of thin air. "Do you think you can adopt the local dialect and accent? Or would that be hard to do?"

"Oh yes," said the merrier of the pair. "I can do it."

"Really?" Arkin smiled a broad, mirthful smile. "Maybe you can help me."

"Yes?"

"I have an old friend who lives here. Or at least, I hope he still lives here."

"Here, in Valparaiso?"

"Yes. We became friends when he came to study in Canada many years ago."

"Yes?"

"I would love to see him again. But he has no idea I'm here, and I'd like to surprise him. He'll shit a brick if I show up at his door."

"A brick?"

"The only problem is all I have is the phone number for his business. I don't have his address."

"I could call the business and ask the address for you," she said, beaming.

Tally-ho. "Yeah, but they might get suspicious."

"What is the business?"

"I'm not even sure. He used to trade in seafood."

The woman thought for a moment. "Maybe I pretend to have a delivery for them."

"But then they would assume you have their address."

"Oh. Yes."

"Hmmm." Arkin feigned deep thought, then a breakthrough. "Hey, how about this? You could tell them part of the shipping label got torn off, and that all you have is their telephone number."

"Yes, that is a good idea. I can do that. Then I ask for their street address. I tell them I call from the postal office. Ah! And I say I have a package from Canada. Then your friend will laugh even more when he sees that his package is his Canadian friend, you."

"That sounds perfect."

"You want me to call now?"

"I think it would be more believable if you call tomorrow morning."

"It will be fun for me."

"Me too," Arkin said, handing her another beer. "Me too."

TWENTY-SEVEN

Twelve restless hours later, Arkin had the street address for the office of a company called Pesquera Mares Verdes, after whoever answered instructed Arkin's Argentine accomplice to "just slip the package through the mail delivery slot in the door" after confirming with her that it contained nothing perishable. He found the office by late morning, doing a quick walk-by to give it a look. To his happy surprise, it turned out to be located barely an eighth of a mile from the hostel, in a row house built of cut stone, midway down a quiet, cobblestoned block. Its tall, antique wooden doorway stood across the street from a coffee house, art gallery, and small restaurant.

He rendezvoused with Morrison in the cemetery again to go over their plan. "The nearest Carabineros police station is only half a mile away from the Pesquera Mares Verdes office as the crow flies," Morrison told him. "But it would take them at least five minutes to get here because it's on a different hill. They have to go down and then back up to get here. Of course, they could already have patrol units operating nearby. It's always a risk."

They stripped themselves of all forms of I.D., caching them behind an overgrown mausoleum. Then they loaded their guns, stuffed them in the beltlines of their pants where they were hidden under their loose-fitting shirts, and set off for the office of Pesquera Mares Verdes.

Since the weather was decent enough, they decided to take turns being outside watching the street—with the other getting to loiter in one of the several businesses on the side of the street opposite the office. Arkin bought a Chilean newspaper and pretended to read it at a window seat in the coffee house, consuming several excellent espressos while he kept watch on the office door. But he didn't spot anyone either coming or going. Morrison joined him after an hour or so.

"How's the coffee?" he asked as he sat down, keeping his eyes looking out the window toward the office's antique front door.

"Mild, but good. Earthy."

"Earthy, he says. The hell does that mean? It tastes like dirt?"

"Try one and see."

A server came and took Morrison's order. An extra-large coffee, black.

"Awful quiet out there," Morrison said.

"Any sense of surveillance?"

"I'm not for sure."

"You're *not for sure*. And the Mississippi dialect rears its ugly head once again."

"You're feeling peppy today. Firing off East Coast elitist insults of the language of my people."

"I dreamt of Hannah last night."

"A good dream, I take it."

"Not a bad one, anyway."

"Was it heavy or spiritual or something?"

"That's the funny thing. It was weird, but seemed entirely frivolous. The two of us were eating banana pancakes at the small table we had in our apartment in Washington, D.C., years ago. Years before we moved to Colorado. Just sitting there reading *The Washington Post*. But the paper was all ads for Dodge pickup trucks and movies with a lot of car chases and explosions, except for one article that said some sort of assembly of ultraconservative Southern evangelicals was pressing for a change to federal regulations that would outlaw the generation of electricity by power plants using anything but coal."

"Huh?"

"Exactly. Anyway, as we ate our dream pancakes and read our dream paper, we were lamenting the fact that the world was being taken over by morons," Arkin shrugged.

"That's it?"

"You were expecting some profound message from the other

side?"

"Knowing your brain, yes, I suppose I was."

Arkin smiled. "The odd thing is, I woke up so happy. A dream of utterly commonplace activity. So ordinary. But it just felt *so real*. So real. Like I'd really had breakfast with her."

Morrison nodded. "Sometimes ordinary is extraordinarily comforting."

"Amen. So why are you *not for sure* about surveillance?"

"Saw a small truck pass by two different times over the course of an hour or so. Slow passes. Strange little truck. More like the front half of a skinny Nissan van with a pickup truck bed attached to it. Looked like some sort of delivery vehicle. White. Plate number EQ-93-74. It didn't stop anywhere that I could see."

"How slow were the passes?"

"Just a hair too slow, you ask me."

"Did you see who was driving?"

"Same driver both times. Guy with a black knit cap. There was a passenger too. But I couldn't see him."

"A panel truck could be making fresh bread delivery runs from the bakery up the street."

"Could be. Probably was. Just thought I'd mention it."

*****

Morrison shifted to the art gallery as Arkin took up position at the far end of the street. An hour later, Morrison came back out to the street as Arkin went to the restaurant, where he ordered a bowl of rice—the cheapest thing he could find on the menu.

A light marine fog settled over Valparaiso as darkness fell. By that time, Arkin sat on a seemingly derelict stoop, pretending to read, by streetlight, a travel book he'd borrowed from the hostel. Still, nobody came or went. The windows that appeared to be those of the address were dark.

He and Morrison met up around the corner.

"I think it's safe to say that nobody is in a big hurry to pick up their mail," Morrison said.

"If any of them are even located in the area, let alone the country," Arkin added, once again beginning to worry that the office was just another voicemail dead letter box. He turned and looked down the street that curved down toward the waterfront, observing a group of three young men who were staggering drunk, shouting things at the night, at nobody in particular—or so it seemed to Arkin. "Screw it," he said.

"What?"

"Let's break in. I didn't see one person go through that doorway all afternoon. It's a Tuesday, isn't it? Not a Chilean national vacation day or anything?"

"You want to break in?"

"What else are we going to do? Sit here for days, maybe weeks, hoping some lackey shows up to get the mail? Go back to your hotel and change into dark clothes. Meet you back here in an hour."

TWENTY-EIGHT

Arkin went back to the hostel, wolfed down an enormous bowl of the house rice and beans in the vacant dining room, then repacked his few belongings, getting them ready to grab from under his bed just in case he had to run for it—though he probably wouldn't even bother returning to the hostel if anything went wrong. Visualizing his approach to the Pesquera Mares Verdes office, running through his planned reactions to the most likely scenarios, he felt the excitement of coming action. This would be his third break-in in less than six weeks. It was almost like the old days.

He pocketed a butter knife from the dining room, donned his baseball cap, pulled it low, and stepped back out into the dark and foggy street. Things were surprisingly quiet, considering it was the dinner hour. The air was still, and he could just detect the scent of someone's cooking nearby. Something sweet, made of yeast dough and dusted with cinnamon.

He met up with Morrison again, and they figured out the best place from which Morrison could keep an eye on the street. There was a clump of bushes and two tiny trees in a small recess fronting one of the colorful row houses half a block down, so Morrison did his best to conceal himself in it.

After making one last scouting pass by the address, strolling down the street with his hands casually jammed into his pockets as if he were on his way to meet friends for a drink, Arkin rounded the block and made his approach. The windows were still dark. He did his best to scan the surrounding area without looking suspicious, mindful of the surprise he had met with in Vancouver. He doubted the group would be expecting him here, unless they'd just happened to catch news coverage of his handiwork at Santiago Airport, and if, against all likelihood, they recognized him from the low-quality security camera footage. Just the same, there was no reason not to be careful.

In a twist of good luck, he found that the office's enormous wooden front door was locked by nothing more than an antique rim latch. He glanced up and down the street, took the butter knife he'd requisitioned from the hostel out of his pocket, and with a quick turn of his wrist, popped the latch from its receiver and opened the door. He slipped in and shut the door behind him, standing still while his eyes adjusted to the dark. The air smelled of beeswax polish and old varnished timbers. He was in a short hallway with a pair of opened doors to either side. Four offices in total. No other exit. It took him barely two minutes to establish that nobody was there, that the offices were apparently abandoned, and that there wasn't a shred of useful evidence from which he could deduce anything. As he'd feared, the place was probably just an address of record for a phone line that automatically forwarded calls to some other number, or went to a remotely-accessed voicemail service, just like the group had set up in Port Hardy, British Columbia, years earlier. All he found was empty wooden desks, rubbish bins with nothing in them but a single chocolate bar wrapper, and haphazard sprinklings of mouse droppings—everything covered in a fine coating of dust.

Damnation.

He didn't want to have to loiter in the area for however long it might take for someone to come collect the mail—assuming anyone would bother. After all he'd been through, it was very possibly another dead end. He put his hands on his hips, let his chin drop to his chest, then exhaled through pursed lips, feeling utterly exhausted and defeated.

*****

Meanwhile, Morrison watched the street from his concealing clump of bushes, realizing, too late, that it was the place where every dog in the neighborhood came to urinate. The stench made his eyes water.

Only one vehicle had passed in the time since Arkin had

disappeared through the front door. A blue Suzuki compact. One new pair of headlights had crested the hillside and was making its way toward him. As it crawled past, Morrison could see that it was a skinny white Nissan half-van, half-pickup truck. It was too dark to read the license plate. But as it reached the address for Pesquera Mares Verdes, it came to a brief stop. It blocked Morrison's view of the door. But a moment later, it resumed its slow roll down the street and then disappeared around a corner.

Shit!

Had it dropped someone off? Had that someone dashed through the door of Pesquera Mares Verdes? He had no way of knowing.

His heart pumping, he broke cover, crossed the street, and speed-walked straight for the door, pulling his pistol from the rear waistband of his pants and racking the slide to put a round into the chamber.

*****

Arkin heard the click of the front door lock as someone outside turned a key. He quickly ducked down behind one of the derelict desks and squatted there, silent, listening. Whomever had come in knew a thing or two about covert movement. Arkin couldn't hear a thing. No footsteps. No breathing. Nothing.

Slowly, silently, he reached back and pulled out his gun, then raised his head until he could just peek over the top of the desk. Before he could see anyone, he was blinded by a muzzle flash from just outside the open doorframe of the office he was in. The clap of the gunshot rang in his ears as a chunk of wood from the desktop splintered and flew against the wall behind him. He dropped back down and rolled to his left as two more gunshots rang out in rapid succession, each sending more splinters of desk wood flying. But then Arkin heard gunshots from farther away. Somewhere closer to the entrance.

Morrison.

There was a rapid exchange of fire—six or seven shots in all—before things went quiet.

"Nate!"

"I'm alright."

"He's down."

Arkin emerged from the back office to find a man flat on his back on the floor, blood pouring from three bullet wounds in his torso, as well as a wound in his face. His lower jaw was gone. Arkin took the man's gun from off the floor, felt for a pulse, then, satisfied he was dead, turned to see Morrison's leg sticking out through the doorframe of one of the other offices.

"Bill?"

"Still with you."

Arkin turned the corner to see Morrison holding a palm against his lower abdomen. "Oh, no!"

"I'll live," Morrison said, gritting his teeth, his voice laden with pain. "But you need to get me to a hospital. Now."

Arkin gave Morrison a quick look. "There's no exit wound. He practically hit the dead center of your lower torso. Why the hell weren't you behind cover?" he asked, unable to help himself.

"I *was* behind cover, jackass. The damned wall is made of quarried stone. Ricochet got me. That's why there's no exit wound."

"In a city of tin and wooden buildings. What luck."

"I think it got me in the bladder."

"Can you stand?"

"With your help."

"Alright. Keep the pressure on it. Try to not let any of your blood drip on the floor. We don't need anyone gathering evidence of your visit. Let's get the hell out of here."

"Search the guy first."

"You sure?"

Morrison nodded, sweat already beading on his hairline and running down his forehead. "Make it quick."

Arkin went back and searched the body, digging through pockets, patting him down. But he found nothing of value. No wallet. No forms of identification. That was telling. A man prepped for covert action. A professional.

Arkin checked the soles of the man's shoes. A few fragments of what looked like sea shell were trapped in a couple of the grooves of the tread. The man's clothes looked Chilean. But the man looked northern European. And from what Arkin could see from his still-intact upper jaw, he was well-to-do—or at least had been at one time. He had expensive, highly professional dental work. His teeth were perfectly straight—an indicator of probable orthodonture. And his front teeth were veneered. Presumably, the man was self-conscious about his appearance.

He helped Morrison to his feet, then helped him shuffle-step back out the front door, scanning up and down the street as he did so, looking for the white van-truck. The street was dead quiet. They crossed it, then made their way down the block to a narrow alley that led to a stairwell down toward the main waterfront road where Arkin knew they'd be able to find a taxi despite the late hour.

Five minutes later, having flagged down a cab and successfully convinced the affable, English-speaking driver that he was helping his drunk friend go visit his ailing mother, Arkin was helping Morrison sit down on a concrete planter in front of the main emergency room doorway of Hospital Carlos van Buren. Then, reluctantly, feeling a tremendous sense of guilt, and with a nod to a thoroughly unhappy looking Morrison, he slipped off into the night.

TWENTY-NINE

The next day, Arkin laid low in the hostel until evening—reasoning that by then the bullet in Morrison's bladder would have been removed, and that he'd be all sewn up and in recovery. Probably on heavy painkillers. But probably—hopefully—coherent. Then, as the sun began to set, he walked the hilly, winding, one-mile route back to Hospital Carlos van Buren, keeping to alleyways and small side-streets wherever possible. Always keeping an eye out for the white Nissan.

Arriving at the hospital, he walked right past the reception desk as if he knew exactly where he was going, then walked the length of the first-floor hall, glancing in each office or room as he went. Not seeing Morrison, he ascended to the second floor via a concrete stairwell at the end of the corridor, then resumed his search.

He found Morrison, at last, in a third-floor room. He had the room to himself. Arkin was somewhat surprised to find that he wasn't handcuffed to the bed, having come in with a gunshot wound. He was asleep. His face a sickly white. There was an IV in his arm. Arkin tried to shrug off a vision of Hannah, attached to an IV, an oxygen cannula in her nose, her skin deathly pale, slowly dying in the hospital back in Durango.

"You look like you could use a foot rub," Arkin said.

Morrison opened his glassy, bloodshot eyes. A weak grin appeared on Morrison's face. "Not from you," he said slowly.

"How are you?"

"It hurts to talk," Morrison said, wincing.

"Ah. Well, I suppose that's the silver lining."

"Funny."

"Actually, you look pretty good for someone who took a bullet to his piss tank."

"Glad it didn't hit any lower."

"In a way, you're quite lucky. I checked that guy's gun. He was loaded with hollow points. If that hole in your belly had been from a direct shot, your lower back would be gone."

"Oh, yes. I feel so very, very lucky," he said, wincing again.

"Are you in pain?"

"Take a wild guess. Good news is they're feeding me some good opiates in this IV drip here. Could be worse."

"Have the police been here?"

"Not that I can recall."

"Then you're doubly lucky," Arkin said, amazed—certain that hospital protocol would require that they notify the police whenever someone arrived with a gunshot wound, and equally certain if the police had found the body at the Pesquera Mares Verdes office, they'd be very curious about anyone showing up at a hospital with a gunshot wound on the same night. Perhaps the police *had* been to the hospital, but when Morrison was unconscious. Perhaps they planned to return. Perhaps they were on their way there right now. At the same time, there was little reason to think the body had been discovered, it being behind locked doors in a derelict office and out of sight. If anyone had found the body at this point, it would have been other operatives of the Priest's group. And it probably would have been in their best interest to make it disappear.

"I assume they already removed the bullet," Arkin said.

"I assume so too. All I know is they put me under and when I woke I was sewn up. Looking forward to another bullet wound scar. Makes it an even four."

"Do they know you're American? Do they know you speak English?"

Morrison closed his eyes and paused for a breath before answering. "Not unless I talked while anesthetized."

"I don't think I should try to move you just yet."

"No."

"What are you going to do?"

"Not speak any English, that's for damned sure. Fake continued semi-consciousness and immobility until I'm well enough to move. Then I'll sneak out."

"Well," Arkin said, pulling a small metal handcuff key from his jacket pocket, "I'm going to leave this with you just in case someone at some point decides your condition is suspicious enough to warrant your restraint." He took a roll of masking tape he'd stolen from the hostel from his other pocket, placed the handcuff key in a piece he tore from the roll, and then stuck the key to the underside of the little side table attached to Morrison's hospital bed.

"Nobody from the group will ever go near that office again," Morrison said.

"Probably not."

"What are *you* going to do now?"

"I don't know. Don't worry about it. Rest. I'll figure it out later." Then he stared down at Morrison, looking regretful. "I suppose I'd better get out of here before somebody comes in and sees me. Can't be known to associate with hooligans like you. I'll check in on you tomorrow evening."

"Okay."

Arkin turned to leave.

"Nate, wait."

"What?"

"Want to know something cool?"

"The hospital serves blue Jell-O?"

"Guess what happened yesterday."

"Besides you getting shot in the bladder?"

"The Colorado River," Morrison said, nearly smiling through his pain.

"What about it?"

"It flowed all the way to the sea."

For a second, Arkin was speechless for reasons he couldn't quite grasp. "The Colorado River? What are you talking about?"

"Forgot to tell you. I read it in *The Durango Herald* online on my phone yesterday just before I left the hotel. They released a bunch of water from a couple of the big dams to restore the flow. Only for a little while. They called it a pulse flow. Still, for a few days, the Colorado will be a real river again."

Arkin paused again, feeling, for a fleeting moment, a strange lightness in his gut. "Thanks for telling me." He looked at Morrison, nodded. "I'll see you tomorrow."

THIRTY

As he left the hospital, sneaking out a back door to avoid the reception area, Arkin felt his sense of guilt and futility returning. Here they were, all the way down south in Chile. Their one lead was now all but certainly a dead end. Morrison was right. Nobody from the Priest's group would ever go near the Valparaiso office again. And they wouldn't be lulled into a trap now that they knew someone was hunting them. All Arkin had accomplished was to spend a bunch of Morrison's money and sick leave hours and get Morrison shot in the bladder. His quest seemed at an end. Yet he couldn't go home. Maybe he'd never be able to go home. And anyway, if he could, it wouldn't change the fact that Hannah had died. He had no one to go back to. It was a disorienting, lonely feeling.

Still, temporary or not, Arkin found the news of the Colorado River reaching the sea strangely comforting. The ancient Colorado—millions of years old—hadn't flowed all the way to the sea in decades, depleted to nothing by ever-increasing demand for irrigation and drinking water. But it did today. And it would again, long after Arkin was gone. Long after humanity was gone. The river would flow once again.

*****

As he walked, Arkin tried to calm his scattered mind with deep breathing exercises. Then, as he neared the hostel, an idea occurred to him. He picked up his pace. Back at the hostel, he un-cached his smartphone and Googled Pesquera Mares Verdes while reprimanding himself for not thinking to do so already.

The search proved difficult, as he expected. The company had no website of its own. The only posted contact information he could locate he found on a business-to-business sales platform for seafood trading companies. The company's posting indicated that it was offering filets of farmed Atlantic salmon for bulk sale, on shipping terms described as "FOB Puerto Cisnes." It provided the same phone number he already had, but no other contact or location information.

Puerto Cisnes?

He continued a long and mostly frustrating search for specific information about the company, hindered by his minimal understanding of Spanish. At last, after following a link he didn't expect to lead anywhere useful, he found a published notice in, of all places, the U.S. Federal Register, documenting the results of an American anti-competitive pricing investigation of Chilean salmon farmers in 1997. Pesquera Mares Verdes was named as a respondent in the case, but there was no contact information for the company. Arkin skimmed the notice twice, then zeroed in on the name of the government agency that oversaw the investigation: the U.S. Department of Commerce. Tracking down the agency's website, Arkin explored it until he found an index of archived document service lists from past investigations. And there, finally, he found a mailing address for the company. At least in 1997, the company received mail at an address in a place called "Isla de los Alemanes."

Island of the Germans? he guessed. A map search revealed it to be a small island, hundreds of miles south of Valparaiso—even well south of Chiloé—in an archipelago to the northwest of Puerto Cisnes. The search also turned up a few photos of the island, apparently shot by touring kayakers, showing shores of weathered rock and expanses of grassy pastureland broken up by clumps of stunted evergreen trees. The only dwellings that could be seen in the photos had walls built of what looked like cut and whitewashed stone, appearing very old. If he hadn't known better, Arkin would have guessed he was looking at photos of sheep farms in Iceland or the northernmost reaches of coastal Sweden.

In the background of a photo of several kayakers on the water, taken, according to the caption, "east of Isla de los Alemanes," stood a towering, snow-capped volcanic peak across a wide body of water.

The volcano was probably on the mainland, in the Andes. It was beautifully symmetrical, with distinctive exposed rock formations near the summit. Two prominent tooth-like spires—basalt, Arkin guessed—protruding through the shimmering glacial cap. "Volcan Melimoyu, across Canal Moraleda," a second line of caption read.

Arkin looked at a satellite image of the island on Google. It looked sparsely populated. There were maybe a dozen farm cottages and small homesteader compounds dotted here and there around the island, half of them looking abandoned. The only significant cluster of buildings was on the northeastern shore, on the leeward side of the island, sheltered from the powerful surf of the open Pacific. The buildings were fronted by a small marina protected by a rectangular breakwater. It looked more like an industrial site than a village, but it probably served as both.

Ten minutes later, Arkin was back in bed. The good news was he wasn't at a complete dead end. The bad news was that the next stop was very, very far away. And he didn't dare approach an airport without a passport. He puzzled over what to do until exhaustion at last took him.

THIRTY-ONE

Arkin woke before dawn with the clear realization that there was no direction to go but forward. He sat up in his bunk—the worn but comfortable mattress tempting him to lie back down, to bundle himself back up in soft, warm blankets, sheltered from the cool, damp predawn air—and sighed. He slid his feet into his cold shoes, slipped out the bunkroom door, down the hall, and into the vacant dining room, where he ate an entire day-old baguette with butter and jam and drank two cups of black tea.

The first thing he wanted to do was go to the hospital to give Morrison the news about finding a possible address for Pesquera Mares Verdes. As he was passing the reception window, he wished the hairy, bohemian-looking overnight clerk a good morning. Arkin hadn't seen him before. His hair was long and dirty, and he wore a brown, hooded alpaca wool sweater. Arkin pegged him as a wannabe anarchist who didn't quite have the necessary resolve.

But as Arkin passed, something in the man's expression caught his eye. Gave him pause. Following his gut instinct, he stopped in his tracks, turned on his heel, and asked the clerk about the weather forecast. But the clerk didn't tell him about the weather.

"Eh . . . ." The clerk looked troubled.

"What is it?"

"There was a man. Last night, a man. Late."

"Yes?"

"He had a fotografía. Photograph. Of you."

"Me?"

"He is looking for you."

"Police?"

"No uniform. Pero—lo siento—but he feels like police."

"Did he say why he was looking for me?"

The man shook his head.

"Are you sure it was me in the photograph?"

"Yes. It was up close, of your face. You are in a suit and tie."

A suit and tie? How long had it been since anyone took a photo of him in a suit and tie? Could it be an old security badge I.D. photo from back in his DCI days? Knowing that the Priest's group had penetrated the upper echelons of DCI, it wasn't out of the realm of possibility.

In the wake of the shootout, it seemed the Priest's group had guessed that Arkin was in Valparaiso. Guessed that it was Arkin who'd killed their operative at the Pesquera Mares Verdes office. It seemed they'd also guessed that he was still staying in a nearby hotel or hostel.

The overnight clerk nodded. A tacit acknowledgement that he was on Arkin's side, if anyone's. He wasn't about to help the police—or anyone who looked like the police. And so far, at least, nobody knew Arkin was staying there.

"Thank you."

"De nada. Take care, my friend."

Arkin went to the front door, paused, and studied the street through the door's glass panes. He didn't see anyone. Not on foot, not sitting in a car. No sign of the white Nissan. He opened the door and stepped out into the gray and rainy Valparaiso morning.

THIRTY-TWO

Arkin once again kept to small side streets and alleyways wherever possible, taking a zig-zagging route through the neighborhood, eyeballing parked cars to make sure there weren't any with passengers sitting in them acting as static surveillance posts. Three moving cars passed him as he walked, and he memorized the color, make, and license plate numbers of each—a black Suzuki hatchback, a silver Hyundai compact, and a gray Volkswagen Kombi. When he was roughly halfway to the hospital, he turned a corner onto a street that had five cars parked along it. Glancing half a block ahead, he spotted one that could have been one of the three that had passed him. It was another silver Hyundai compact. He couldn't see the license plate yet. But as he drew nearer, it became clear that two men were sitting in it.

Arkin stopped short and felt his front pockets as though it had just occurred to him to look for his keys. Then he turned around and headed in the opposite direction, not daring to look behind him, but scanning everything in front of him, looking for any indicators of surveillance or pursuit. As he passed a shop that had a door recessed in a glass entryway, he checked the reflection to see what was going on behind him. The silver Hyundai was on the move, approaching him from behind. But now there was only the driver. That meant the passenger was on foot somewhere.

Arkin came to an alleyway footpath that split the block. He turned onto it. And as soon as he was out of sight of the silver Hyundai, he took off running for all he was worth. The footpath emerged on the far side of the block, then crossed another street and continued through the middle of the next block, descending two short staircases as it did so. But as Arkin crossed the street, his eye was drawn to movement. A man was running down the street toward him—presumably the passenger from the silver Hyundai. When Arkin was halfway through the next block, he glanced back to see the man in pursuit, a few dozen yards behind him.

Arkin turned right at the next street, only to see the silver Hyundai come racing around the corner. He stopped, turned around, then sprinted toward the top of a stairwell he saw at the opposite end of the street where it made a sharp turn and disappeared around a corner. Reaching it at full speed, he jumped, flying over the first eight steps before making a hard landing and nearly losing his balance before resuming his flight. The walkway he was now on appeared to be heading toward the abrupt edge of the hilltop neighborhood—toward the bluff where the land dropped away, down to streets paralleling the waterfront. As he neared the edge, he saw that the path made a hard left turn. As soon as he made the turn, he spotted the recessed doorway of a small wooden house fronting the footpath along the edge of the drop-off, its porch in the shadow of a wooden overhang. He stopped in his tracks, then ascended the three short steps up into the dark recessed doorway. There he crouched, spring-loaded for action, listening. A moment later, he heard his pursuer's footfall as he ran toward the same sharp turn at the edge of the drop-off. As soon the man made the turn and was about to cross in front of Arkin's hiding place, Arkin sprang forward, keeping low. The man saw Arkin, but not with enough time to react. Arkin, flying out nearly horizontal to the ground, hit the man hard in the pelvis, putting his full momentum and weight behind his right shoulder, driving into the man as if he were a tackling dummy. An ornate, 3-foot-tall concrete barrier was all that lined the edge of the path. His own speed now his own greatest enemy, the man twisted sideways and flailed to regain his balance as he flew at a diagonal toward the barrier. It hit him low, below the waist, and wasn't enough to stop him. He disappeared over the edge without making a sound. Arkin took two seconds to breathe and look up and down the path to make sure there hadn't been any pedestrian witnesses. Then he looked over the edge. The man had landed mid-torso on top of a concrete wall three stories down. His body was folded in half over the top of it. He was probably dead. If not, he was clearly unconscious and would certainly never walk again.

Then a glint of metal caught Arkin's eye. There was an object on the roof of a building just inside the wall. It was about the size of a cell phone. Arkin felt his pocket. *Oh, shit.* It must have come loose in the melee, as he pushed his pursuer over the edge of the cliff. There was no apparent way to recover it, short of stealing a 30-foot ladder. He'd have to do without.

THIRTY-THREE

Arkin was able to hail a taxi to run him back to the hostel and then wait while he gathered his belongings. Returning to the still-vacant dining room, he stuffed all the remaining food items on the breakfast table—bread, butter, peanut butter, packets of sugar, instant coffee and tea—into the clean plastic garbage bag he'd pulled from the room's rubbish bin. Placing his bag of food by the door, he slipped back into the dark bunk room, allowed his eyes to adjust for a moment, listened for evidence that anyone might be awake, and then grabbed his bag, as well as the largest backpack he could find among the gear of his seven fellow bunkroom guests. Moving quickly, he made for the exit, stuffing the food bag into the backpack as he opened the front door and stepped out into the street.

His first priority was to get out of the immediate area. He had the cab drive him north, along the waterfront, on Avenida España, as he pondered his options. He had no valid passport. He was a wanted man in both hemispheres of the New World. There was no option but to go forward, into the unknown.

After a couple of miles, Arkin spotted a small marina full of sailboats. Stealing a boat had helped him cross from British Columbia to Washington State when he escaped arrest in Vancouver. And it was looking like a good option once again.

He felt bad abandoning Morrison. But Morrison could handle himself, if anyone could. Given that the only blood left behind in the office of Pesquera Mares Verdes was that of one of Priest's group's operatives, Arkin was able to convince himself that the group had little reason to guess Morrison might be in a hospital. For that matter, they probably didn't have any reason to think Morrison was in Chile. Morrison also had a handcuff key, as well as tremendous skills in manhandling people. And, at least with respect to his bullet wound, he was probably out of danger. In any event, Arkin didn't think he could afford to wait around in Valparaiso. The Priest's group would keep hunting him. And even if they couldn't find him, his photo would surely find its way into the hands of the police and the local news. It was just too dangerous.

The city was slowly coming to life. He had the cab driver drop him at the nearest supermercado, where he spent most of his remaining cash on cheap, sustaining staples—beans, rice, salt, and bottled water. Then he found a bench in a tiny park across the street, sat down, and watched other patrons exiting the store. Before long, he saw what he was looking for. An overweight, middle-aged woman in what Arkin guessed was a housekeeper's uniform. She pushed a wheeled cart loaded with food out the door, down the sidewalk, and into the neighborhood. Having stowed his own groceries in his new backpack, Arkin rose and began to follow her at a discreet distance. Within a few minutes, she stopped under an old eucalyptus tree at the foot of a steep stairwell leading up to a spectacular home of whitewashed stone and tall curved windows, its sloping yard immaculately landscaped and enclosed by an old black wrought iron fence. She pulled two grocery bags from the cart, and began her climb to the house. As soon as she disappeared through the door, Arkin made a quick pass by the cart, grabbing all four of the remaining grocery bags.

*****

Half an hour later, under a tree in a small waterfront park, Arkin took inventory of his haul. In addition to the groceries he'd purchased himself, he had a dozen apples, two cartons of orange juice, a loaf of white bread, a jar of honey, a bag of white potatoes, two yellow onions, and two tins of smoked oysters. He also had a pair of polyester shorts that were too big for him, as well as a couple of cotton T-shirts, a fleece pullover, a safety razor, and a light waterproof jacket, all compliments of his former bunkmate.

Reorganized and repacked, he made his way down to the small

marina he'd spotted from the cab and cased the available vessels before settling on a sturdy but neglected—and therefore, hopefully, infrequently used—Coronado 30. Probably at least 40 years old, but solid. Breaking into the cockpit, he was happy to see an autopilot and an old VHF radio hooked up to one of two marine batteries. The batteries appeared to be wired to a mount for a solar panel, but the panel was missing. There was a small stove, but no water maker. *Well, if I need water, I'll just put in somewhere*, he thought. He turned on the radio to confirm that at least one of his batteries held a charge. It would have been nice to have a GPS receiver. But Arkin figured he'd avoid getting lost by simply staying within 30 or 40 miles of the Chilean coast. All he would really ever have to do is turn the boat until the compass read 'east,' and he'd see land sooner or later.

There was no gas for the small outboard—which wasn't ideal, but he had no time to be picky—so he raised the mainsail and used the breeze to back out of the slip. A minute later, he was underway, heading through the gap in the breakwater, slipping out into the open Pacific.

THIRTY-FOUR

Though he sailed against southerly winds and the cold Humboldt Current, Arkin covered a good distance with fair seas his first four days at sail, tacking his way back and forth down the coast. It occurred to him that going against the current, sailing into the wind, was becoming the story of his life.

There were two minor disappointments. One came in his discovery that the stove was out of propane so that he had to eat cold food. No big deal. The other was that he couldn't figure out how to work the Spanish language autopilot control. That meant that, barring extraordinarily consistent wind, he had to man the helm whenever he was underway, and had to drop sail when he wanted to sleep. It would slow him down, but wasn't the end of the world.

On his second day out of Valparaiso, a Chilean Coast Guard inshore patrol boat made a close pass. But Arkin waved confidently as it went by, pleased with himself that he'd had the foresight to fly the small Chilean ensign he'd found in the cabin from the short flagstaff mounted on the transom. One of the crew appeared to study him through binoculars for a minute or so. But the vessel continued on its way without altering course. Nevertheless, worried by the encounter, Arkin changed his heading to take himself farther offshore, reasoning that it would lessen his chances of coming across another Coast Guard vessel, or anyone else who might identify either him or his stolen boat. Sailing farther from land had its own set of risks. But he was more confident in his ability to manage the seas than he was in his chances of not being recognized nearer the coast. Plus, he had plenty of food and water to hold him for a while if anything went wrong. By evening, he was out of sight of land.

That night, when Arkin woke to the urge to urinate, he emerged from the cabin to witness the brightest shooting star he had ever seen. A bright white fireball trailing an eerie green tail clear across the sky, from south to north. It didn't hurt that it was one of the darkest nights he'd ever experienced, with no moon and no visible light pollution. Seeing the meteorite filled him with a sense of wonder, so he sat awake for a good hour, staring up at the Milky Way and studying the unfamiliar constellations of the Southern Hemisphere, eventually spotting the Southern Cross. It was the first time he'd ever seen it. And though it was ludicrous given the circumstances, he began to hum the Crosby, Stills, and Nash song about seeing the same constellation. He reflected on just how unpredictable and insane life could be.

*****

On his fifth day at sea, the wind began to shift to westerly, then northwesterly, and with the shift came a growing swell. For the next 12 hours, it was manageable—nothing he hadn't handled before—though it made sleeping in the rolling cabin almost impossible. But the wind and swells continued to grow, and the boat began to heel so much that he had to lower his foresail and double-reef his main. Worse, to guard against taking a rogue wave over the beam, he had to keep altering his course farther and farther to the west, out to sea. He stowed his food and water in a couple of latched cupboards above the agonizingly tempting sleeping berth, took the extra measure of lashing the cupboard doors shut with a scrap piece of duplex marine wire he'd found on the floor, and then secured the door to the cabin. By evening, it was clear to an exhausted, sleep-deprived Arkin that, even though the waves were still sinusoidal, he would have to stay at the helm in case they began to break.

*****

Sure enough, shortly after midnight, the waves did start to break. Arkin lashed himself to the captain's chair with a spare halyard. Fatigued and dying for sleep as he was, he knew that if he faltered now, if he let go the helm for even a few seconds, he could, in the blink of an eye, turn to take one of the huge waves abeam and capsize. To guard against that, he was making constant adjustments to keep the bow headed into the waves, squinting to discern their direction in the dim starlight, fighting the wheel. He wondered how tall the waves were, worrying that if they got much higher, they could pitch-pole his boat, sending it end over end. He wished he'd had the forethought to rig some sort of improvised sea anchor from the jib sail. But it was too late for that, as he didn't dare let go of the wheel. He hadn't slept more than an hour in the last grueling day-and-a-half, and began to fear that he might simply fall unconscious from exhaustion.

Waves crashed over the bow, one after the other, relentless, cold, soaking Arkin to the skin. After heading nose-in to one of the largest waves yet, the boat popped out the other side at such an angle that the rudder was momentarily raised out of the water, just long enough for the boat to be turned a few more degrees off the swell. Before Arkin could regain control, the boat took a wave largely abeam, and rolled to the point where he hung in the air, dangling from the halyard that lashed him to the seat. As his feet flailed about trying to find the deck before the boat righted itself, he heard a loud crash from inside the cabin. Engaged as he was in managing the boat, he couldn't go below to see what had caused it. But he had a bad feeling and worried through the night, listening as whatever had come loose continued to clunk around in the cabin as the boat listed this way and that.

*****

To his considerable surprise, Arkin survived the night. And shortly before dawn, the swell began to recede. By mid-morning, the seas, while still rough, had subsided to the point that Arkin thought it more-or-less safe to heave-to and go below for what he imagined would be the best sleep of his life. Under normal circumstances, he wouldn't have risked it. But there was nothing normal about his state of exhaustion. Plus, he was aching with hunger and thirst.

Going below at long last, he was chagrined to find that the crash and clunking sounds he'd heard through the night had come from his water jugs. The hinges of one of the high cupboard doors had detached from the flimsy, brittle wood to which they'd been screwed, and Arkin's water jugs had, one and all, broken through and fallen out.

They were spread out over the floor, dented and broken open. He was almost too tired to care. He did what he could to direct the last few sips from each jug into his mouth, refusing to panic, reasoning that he'd simply sail east toward the coast as soon as he woke up. There, he'd find a place to drop anchor, go ashore, and find water. Despite being forced to head farther out to sea to contend with the storm, he figured he couldn't be more than a day's sail from land. He knew from his Marine Corps survival training that he could go a few days without water. No problem. He opened a tin of smoked oysters, dumped them, oil and all, onto a slice of bread, folded it in half, and devoured it in three bites. Then he lashed himself to a berth and passed out, still in his soaking wet clothes.

THIRTY-FIVE

Arkin woke up 18 hours later in predawn darkness under a canopy of bright stars. The sea was calm. Dead calm. He was parched. And as the eastern sky slowly lightened, he realized he was also out of sight of land—even the high mountaintops of the Andes—with no real idea of how far he was from the coast. Still, he refused to panic. The weather would change. The wind would surely pick up as the day wore on.

As the sun popped over the horizon, he decided to check the condition of the VHF radio. He'd had the foresight to dismount it from the console and put it in the cabin before the storm got out of hand. But, like the water jugs, it had fallen to the floor. Then it had slid to a corner and come to rest directly under a trickle of rainwater that leaked in through the top of the cabin doorjamb throughout the storm. It shouldn't have mattered, given that it was a presumably water-tight maritime radio of a respectable brand name that Arkin recognized. But when he hooked it back up to the battery and turned it on, it didn't work. Perhaps the circuitry had been damaged as it was knocked about in the storm. Perhaps it was a cheap counterfeit that wasn't really waterproof. Whatever the case, it wasn't good. He removed the cover to find water droplets on the wiring. He shook them out as best he could and set the open radio in a sunny spot on the deck, hoping the problem was simply water inundation, and that it might eventually dry out and work again.

As the sun rose higher in the sky, the air began to grow hot. It was, after all, nearly summer in the Southern Hemisphere. Arkin went below to get out of the direct sun, but soon found that the temperature in the cabin was climbing above what it was outside. He rigged the Genoa sail over a section of the deck as a sunshade, then lay in the shadow beneath it in his underwear with nothing to do but wait. His thoughts returned to the question of how long he could go without water. What was it they taught him in the Marines? Five days at best? No. Not this time. Given the heat, as well as the quantity of body water he'd surely lost in his exertions through the storm, less. Maybe four days. Maybe.

It occurred to Arkin that there could be potable water in bilge compartments below the cabin floor, including at least some of what had spilled from his jugs. He went below and pulled up the only floor hatch he could find. Hallelujah! There was water. Maybe three gallons sloshing around in the bottom of the reservoir. A rainbow sheen of oil floated on its surface. But Arkin figured that if push came to shove, he could rig some sort of straw to draw water from below the oil slick. And even if he drank a little oil, he'd still be better off than if he had no water at all. Hopeful, he dipped a cupped hand and drew it up to his nose. It smelled of saltwater. He stared down at it, frowning, then let the hatch drop with a bang.

Hour upon hour he lay on the deck, thirsty, a mouthful of cotton, waiting for the wind. For a breeze. For anything. He hadn't urinated in at least a day and had no hint of an urge to. He ate his two remaining oranges for their moisture, but they didn't put a dent in his thirst. And as soon as he finished them, his mouth was dry again, his tongue tacky, feeling swollen. In a moment of fleeting hope, it occurred to him that he could fashion some sort of condenser to boil fresh water from the salt water. But then he remembered the stove was out of propane.

*****

A day and a half passed. The occasional gentle lapping against the hull taunted him. The sound of water. Such an abundance of water, all around him. But all of it poison. To ingest even a cupful would draw the water remaining in his cells down below the critical level at which the cells would begin to die. He hoped that, if he began to lose his grip, the temptation of the sight and sounds of water wouldn't overcome his awareness that a drink of it would seal his fate.

He made a makeshift rain-catcher out of the jib sail, shaping it into a broad funnel that would direct water down into a plastic bucket he'd found in the cabin. But overhead, the sky was as blue and clear as any he'd ever seen. There wasn't so much as a single puff of cloud from horizon to horizon.

Seeking comfort in normal life routine, he wet his face with saltwater and gave himself a rough shave with the safety razor he'd stolen from his hostel bunkmate. Though he had no mirror, he pictured his cheeks starting to sink inward, the tissue starved for water. He convinced himself he was being silly. He hadn't been that long without water. His cheeks were fine. He was fine.

At the end of the day, he reassembled the radio, attached it to the marine battery, and flipped the on-switch. It was still dead. He figured its components would have dried off by now. Perhaps the problem wasn't moisture. Perhaps the fall had simply damaged it beyond repair. Regardless, Arkin disassembled it once again and set the components out to dry further, though they weren't visibly wet anymore. It was worth a shot.

*****

Toward the end of his second waterless day, Arkin's mind began to obsess over his location. Specifically, he wondered how far west he'd sailed during the storm, and which direction the current was taking him. For all his previous efforts to avoid other vessels, he began to wish he were near the main shipping lanes. The invisible highway containerships and other vessels took as the most direct and fuel-efficient route between Cape Horn and the major Chilean ports of Antofagasta, Valparaiso, and Talcahuano. Perhaps an enormous Korean or Dutch-flagged vessel would scoop him out of the sea and spirit him off to some distant land where he wasn't wanted and where he could regroup and renew his quest. But, in all likelihood, he'd sailed and drifted well to the west-north-west of the shipping lanes. Indeed, he hadn't seen so much as a distant mast or running light in two days. More disconcerting still, he hadn't seen a single living creature. No whales, seals, or jumping fish. Not even any birds. It was as if he'd drifted into some sort of maritime dead zone. A pelagic wasteland. A desert.

"What was it that Paul Shepard said?" he asked out loud, trying to redirect his thoughts. "To the desert go prophets and hermits; through deserts go pilgrims and exiles. Here the leaders of the great religions have sought therapeutic and spiritual values of retreat, not to escape, but to find reality." This trackless sea is a desert, he thought. But it's not my destination. It's just another leg of the journey of another exile.

Realizing that the lack of activity and the heavy silence were starting to get to him, he decided to do a few yoga moves Hannah had once taught him after badgering him into trying them out as a way to reduce stress. The sun salutation, the downward dog, and a couple of others with names he couldn't recall—though he clearly remembered thinking the names were ludicrous. But doing it reminded him of Hannah, making him sad, so he stopped after a few minutes.

Around midday, he reassembled and turned on the radio again. It still didn't work. As he tried to keep his mind occupied, his eyes scanned the horizon to the east, straining to see any hint of land. In all directions, the glass-calm sea stretched to the absolute limits of his vision. He maintained his watch until the glare of unobstructed sunlight made his head hurt, forcing him to take a break. He tied a shirt into a Bedouin style keffiyeh headdress, drew it around his face to give his eyes a break from the glare, and resumed his watch.

THIRTY-SIX

Another day came and went, and Arkin's control over his conscious mind began to flag. Unwelcome thoughts began to intrude, no matter how hard he tried to focus on other things. His biggest mistake had been in trying to picture the future—a future in which he was alive and back on land. It was another trick they'd taught him in one of his numerous survival courses. To stave off despair, visualize the future with you alive in it. The problem—the landmine—triggered with trying this trick was the unavoidable observation that Hannah was gone. As he tried to picture the future, her absence made it altogether sad and empty. He didn't want to think about the future. But having done so, he'd had to burn considerable emotional and mental energy to turn away from it again. Somehow, the effort had cost him dearly. Somehow, this had worn him down, made his mind more vulnerable.

At one point, he actually considered praying. But after giving it serious thought—even forming the first lines of prayer in his head—he laughed out loud at his own hypocrisy. Him, an avowed atheist who prided himself on basing his understanding of the universe around him on facts and reason. He laughed again as he pictured himself on his knees, deep in prayer. Ridiculous. Still, the idea stuck with him far longer than he cared to acknowledge.

*****

Around the middle of his fourth waterless day, Arkin was wavering between hope and despair. Clichés began to pop into his mind. *This too shall pass. But will it, really? I'm so tired. Easier to say to hell with it and quit fighting. No, no—what was it Churchill said? When you're in Hell, keep going. Or something like that. But keep going where? And what difference will it make? Hannah is gone.*

It came to him that he could turn his sorrow back into anger, and that the anger could possibly sustain him. Hannah died alone because of the group. Pratt died because of the group. His career and former life died because of the group. *When I find them, I will destroy them. I will kill every last one of them.*

Then he caught a brief glint of reflected sunlight out of the corner of his eye. He turned and stared in the direction from which he thought it had come. But there was nothing there. Nothing but empty sea, clear to the far eastern horizon. *Wait!* It flashed again. *A ship!* A ship reflecting the light of the sun. His heart pounded. What to do? His sails were up and a radar reflector was installed high on his backstay. He could think of no other way to make himself more noticeable to anyone aboard the ship who might be on watch and using binoculars or radar. He had no means of signaling his distress. No flares, no flags, nothing with which to make a smoke column. Not even a mirror. He continued to stare. At length, though it remained many miles away, the vessel drew close enough that he could make out its basic shape. It was, of all things, a cruise ship.

Arkin imagined a vigilant lookout catching sight of him through his powerful binoculars, deducing the direness of his situation, and alerting his captain that a rescue was in order. Arkin imagined him using the antiquated but charming language typical of the British Royal Navy during the Napoleonic Wars, much as it was described in Patrick O'Brian's Master and Commander novels. "On deck, there! Sail, ho! Three points off the starboard bow." Salvation. And a cup of tea with the captain.

But it was not to be. Arkin watched the ship progress southward with surprising speed, from one corner of the horizon to the other, all the while desperately willing it to change course, watching for the slightest change of heading. None came. As it steamed farther and farther away, he pictured what might be happening onboard. Passengers in swimsuits lazily kicking around in the enormous freshwater pool of the sundeck. Passengers sipping from large glasses of cola served over ice. Lemonade. Pure, fresh water. Passengers eating from large platters stacked high with juicy slices of ripe fruit that Arkin could almost smell and taste—bright yellow pineapple, orange mango and papaya, green kiwi, red strawberries. Passengers happily sweating away some of the bounty of fresh water carried in their bodies. A bounty of water they all took for granted. Water available in abundance, 24/7 and on-demand, piped to every conceivable corner of their massive, comfortable ship from giant tanks concealed within. Giant tanks of fresh water, now disappearing below the southeastern horizon.

By sunset, Arkin was sure his heart was beating faster than normal despite his being utterly inactive. As darkness fell, the air grew cold. Mercifully, he fell asleep just after nightfall and slept until dawn.

THIRTY-SEVEN

The next day, he woke to find that the sea was still dead calm. He kicked his empty water bottles across the floor and slammed the hatch as he emerged from the cabin before realizing his irritability was probably a side-effect of his worsening dehydration. His heart rate was still elevated. He felt hung over. His sense of desperation grew as he took stock of his situation. He wouldn't last much longer. And again, the relentless, blazing sun was, with each passing second, climbing higher and higher into the sky.

Hardly believing it was worth the effort, he reassembled the radio once again, hooked it up to the marine battery, and turned it on. *Static!* It was working. There was hope.

He had to do a few breathing exercises to calm himself before he could turn the frequency dial slowly enough to scan for chatter. Regaining his composure, he turned the dial in micro adjustments, roughly two-tenths of a megahertz at a time, pausing, then another two-tenths, and so on up the frequency range. He ran through the full frequency spectrum four times. Nothing. Nobody. Not knowing how much battery power he had left, he decided to switch off and try again every hour or so.

Hour upon hour, he ran through his radio check, beginning with a renewed sense of hope, but ending each check with a little less hope than before. By evening, he began to despair once again. For all he knew, he was hundreds of miles offshore, out of the commercial shipping lanes and far from any fishing grounds, beyond radio range of anyone who might be listening, out where the South Pacific was a great blue nothing.

He was growing lethargic. Before long, he knew, he would go into shock. And that would be it. Maybe they would find his desiccated body, still aboard, off the shore of New Zealand or Fiji. Maybe the current would push him north, to Peru. To Ecuador. Maybe they would find and bury him in the Galapagos Islands. Darwin's islands. A place Arkin had always thought of as a happy symbol of a quantum leap forward in human reason. There were worse places one could be buried.

At one point, lying on his back on the deck under the radio, he tore open the oppressive silence by breaking into song. An old favorite, Pink Floyd's melancholy *Wish You Were Here*.

"So, so you think you can tell, Heaven from Hell, blue skies from pain...."

He stopped as he ran out of energy. A few moments later, he chuckled for no reason he could fathom, then resumed singing, skipping to the song's refrain as he pictured Hannah sitting under a palm tree on a remote Hawaiian beach years before, smiling and healthy.

"We're just two lost souls swimming in a fish bowl, year after year." Deep breath. "Running over the same old ground. What have we found? The same old fears. Wish you were here." He rested his head on the bare deck and silence descended once again.

*****

The last deep red band of the sunset faded on the western horizon and the sky grew dark. Darker than normal. Arkin's vision was tunneling, his consciousness beginning to flag. He lay down close to the radio so that he wouldn't have to exert any more energy than necessary to use it.

He began to reflect on how he'd come to be here, dying of thirst on the open sea. The chain of events was too ludicrous to believe. In his banishment to a remote, sparsely populated corner of the Mountain West, had he really crossed the path of an old, invisible adversary? A hidden puppet master who'd driven him from his career, from his dying wife's bedside, from his home? And now, having been shot, having escaped arrest twice, having chased meager scraps of evidence halfway around the world, was he doomed to die of mere dehydration?

Was the Priest's group even down here? If he somehow survived to complete his journey, would he find nothing more than a remote fish-farming operation, staffed by innocent Chileans mystified that a worn down and weather-beaten gringo would travel thousands of miles to see what they were up to? He could picture their faces, eyeballing him, perplexed. If he'd had the energy, he would have laughed. The whole thing was insane. And he was insane to have come this far. Exhausted, he let his heavy eyelids close.

*****

I'll let you in on a little secret, Nathaniel, his childhood pediatrician in Manhattan was telling him as he sat on a paper-covered vinyl bed in an examination room wearing nothing but white briefs. *You can drink seawater.*

Really?

Yes. All that stuff about seawater dehydrating you is just urban legend.

It is?

Definitely. In fact, they finally figured out that the rumor was started by a ring of municipal water utility executives from the bigger coastal cities. New York, Miami, Los Angeles, Seattle, and so on. They were all in on it. Bunch of fat cats brainwashing us into thinking we need their product. The doctor shook his head in disgust.

A conspiracy.

Exactly. So drink up. I know how thirsty you are. How parched. Try a cup. It's nice and cold. The extra electrolytes are good for you.

That sounds really good. Really refreshing.

Go ahead then.

Okay.

*****

It what seemed the blink of an eye, but could have been hours, Arkin came to in darkness. *Am I dead?* As his eyes adjusted, he saw that he was still in the boat, that it was still night, and that, thankfully, there was no evidence—no nearby cup, no little puddles, no wet clothing—to indicate that he'd tried to drink seawater.

Certain it was a futile final gesture, he lifted a weak arm to switch the radio on and turn the dial to scan frequencies once more. But there was still nothing to hear. Nothing at all. Listening to the empty hiss of the receiver as he lay there in the dark, he realized he'd never felt so utterly isolated and alone in his entire life.

Having reached the upper end of the frequency range, he started back down, with barely the energy to turn the dial between his index finger and thumb. Nothing, nothing, nothing. Then, a burst of static, as though someone were keying a microphone. Was he dreaming? Another burst of static. Then voices. Distant, distorted by static. But voices nonetheless. A far away conversation between several boats. Probably fishing boats radioing activity and position reports to each other. But he couldn't make out what they were saying in their quick Spanish. Wait—was it Spanish? The accents sounded South American. Yet Arkin wasn't sure he'd heard any Spanish words. But what other language could it be? Arkin mustered all the strength he could to sit up. He took a deep breath, grabbed the microphone, and in broken Spanish made worse by his cottonmouth, shouted "Emergencia! Emergencia! I have no agua. No agua."

For a few lonely moments, the channel went utterly silent. Arkin's heart sank. Perhaps he had been hallucinating after all. Finally, one of the boats responded.

"Que? Repita para mí, por favor."

If the voices hadn't been speaking Spanish before, they certainly were now.

"Emergencia. No agua."

" ¿Quién es esto? ¿Como te llamas?"

Arkin didn't give his name, but did his best to explain, in English, where he thought he might be: 100 or 200 kilometers southwest of Concepción. A wild guess, at best.

"¿Donde?" the perplexed sounding voice asked.

He couldn't be sure, but he thought the voice instructed him, in halting and broken English, to key his microphone every few minutes. Did one of them have an automatic direction finder they could tune to his VHF radio frequency? He'd practiced using such devices back in Recon training, but had no idea whether they were common equipment on boats. It seemed unlikely. Maybe he was misunderstanding them, or hallucinating what he wanted to hear. In any case, he fought to keep his eyes open, fought to stay conscious, the darkness ever closing in around him.

Every few minutes, he keyed the mic. But his body and mind were failing. He had the sensation he was sinking into the deck of the boat as he lay on his back. Then he got the spins. Then, gradually, he lost consciousness.

THIRTY-EIGHT

Back in Valparaiso, hundreds of miles to the north, Morrison opened his eyes after pretending to be asleep as the night nurse peeked through a crack in the door to check on him. Earlier in the day, they'd finally removed the leads to the vital- signs monitor from his body. He'd waited for this day for a long time—both because the vitals monitor would have chimed with an alarm if he'd removed the leads while it was still on, and because he had to come far enough in his recovery from bladder surgery that he could walk. But now he was ready.

Morrison reached under the side table and pulled the handcuff key Arkin had left for him from the tape that held it to its hiding place. To his continued amazement, no police had ever showed up to handcuff him to the bed—let alone ask him any questions. But he decided to hang onto the key just in case he ran into any trouble down the road, concealing it in the bottom of his sock.

Quickly, he got dressed, slipped his shoes on, opened his door a crack to see if the coast was clear, and slipped out. He made straight for the fire escape, took it all the way to the ground floor, then went out the door and disappeared into the crisp Valparaiso night.

As he walked as quickly as he could with a good bit of residual pain in his abdomen, he wondered what had happened to Arkin. He hadn't had a visit in several days. Had some new piece of evidence come to light that obliged him to rush off? Had he been arrested? Had he been killed? Morrison figured Arkin would have left him a message on his cell phone.

When Morrison finally made it to his hotel, the front desk clerk gave him his suitcase and a small cardboard box into which they'd put loose articles they'd found in his room when they finally went in to clean it out—not having known what became of him. He powered up his phone and checked for messages. There were none. He dialed Arkin's number. He got some sort of recording. He couldn't understand the Spanish, but guessed it was telling him that the person he was dialing was not available. He couldn't even leave a voicemail.

If Arkin was still alive, he was on his own.

THIRTY-NINE

Arkin thought he heard something mechanical. A deep hum. *A diesel boat engine? Could it be?* But when he opened his eyes, he found himself enveloped in a cold, dark, gray void of howling wind, empty but for the towering figure he stood toe-to-toe with. Once again, it was the Anasazi priest from the pictograph he'd found near the Animas River while fishing with Morrison and Pratt what seemed like years ago. The priest who inhabited his dreams.

He stood at least eight feet tall, and his face was tipped forward to look down on Arkin. There were no discernable arms or legs—only a broad-shouldered monolith of a torso. Yet his body seemed more shadow than anything corporeal. A figure comprised of dark emptiness. The only parts of him that looked like something physical were his glowing red eyes. But behind them, there was nothing.

He inhabits this ethereal plane, Arkin thought with a sense of heartened wonder. *He waits for me here. Maybe there is more to the universe after all. No. I'm hallucinating.*

Still, with a flicker of hope, he whispered, "Bryant," then slowly reached out to touch the figure—to touch its absence of light. But as his hand seemed about to make contact with the priest's body, the wind rendered the priest to dust. The void went dark and Arkin had the sensation he was falling backward into nothingness.

*****

Arkin smelled plumeria.

"Nathaniel. Nathaniel, wake up."

Hmmm?

"Wake up."

It was Hannah's voice. *Hannah?*

Arkin opened his eyes to find himself slumped on a wooden bench, leaning with his back against an unfinished plywood wall. He was in a dark, narrow, unadorned wooden house, a single naked light bulb scarcely illuminating the room from its socket on an exposed rafter overhead. The floor was concrete slab, bare but for one dark area rug of a style that reminded him of the rug in Lily Bryant's house. The close air smelled of fried onions and baking pastry. Two children sat on another bench against the opposite wall. They looked Native American. They were staring at him, silent.

"Did you see the priest?" Arkin asked.

The children looked at each other, then back at him, expressionless.

"The priest. Was he here?"

Arkin's head spun. He wondered if he wasn't seeing a vision of the afterlife. Perhaps he'd died of dehydration on the boat, and had now come to the place to which the Anasazi had vanished so many centuries earlier.

The children continued to stare. Arkin closed his tired eyes once again.

*****

When he next came into light, he was staring at a lone cliff dwelling tucked up under the lip of a shallow canyon ridge above a river that might have been the Animas. It was after sundown, the light rapidly waning. A purple-edged veil of darkness was approaching from the east at unnatural speed. He was only a few feet from the short doorway of the ancient sandstone structure. But strain as he might, he couldn't make out anything in the pitch-dark interior. As he stared, a figure approached the door from within and emerged, meeting his eyes. It was Hannah. Her skin was glowing. She had all her beautiful dark hair again. She was wearing her favorite white linen dress and silver Harvey bracelets on her wrists.

"Hannah?" he asked in a desperately sad voice. My wife is dead. I'm dreaming a cruel dream. This isn't real. Is this real? "What were you doing in there?"

But she didn't speak. She just nodded and smiled. It was the same heartwarming smile that, all on its own, used to pull Arkin out of his fits of despair and set him back on his feet again, reassured that there were good things, good people in the world.

She stepped forward, took his hands in hers, then stared into his eyes for a moment. Holding her warm hands, Arkin changed his mind. This was real. He opened his mouth to speak, but she put a finger to his lips to keep him quiet, then leaned forward and kissed him. Before he could react, she turned and, keeping hold of one of his hands, led him back toward the dark doorway of the cliff dwelling. But he grew afraid and stood firm. She turned and looked at him and smiled again. Her lips didn't move, but in his head he heard her say, "Come with me."

"What's in there?"

She smiled that glowing, all-powerful smile again, and he relented. He stepped forward and followed her into the darkness.

*****

With a thud, he woke to find himself lying on his side on the dirt floor of what looked like a plywood storage shed, his eyes wet with tears. Dirt-caked farming tools lined one wall. Parts of three honeybee hives sat in a corner. He lay alongside a cot he guessed he'd fallen off of. His jacket hung over the back of a small wooden chair. Next to where his head had landed was a large jug of water and a plate with what looked like two empanadas on it.

He had a splitting headache and felt like shit from head to toe. Much worse than the worst hangover of his life. He wiped his arm over his face to dry the tears and grunted as he sat up on his elbows, blinking to clear his eyes. There was a pale light in the sky outside a small window above the tools. It was either a little while before dawn or after sunset. He had no idea what time it was, or, for that matter, where he was. The last thing he remembered was hearing people speaking in an unrecognizable language on the boat's radio as he began slipping into shock.

What the hell?

He sat up, leaning against the cot, trying to get his bearings. The empanadas smelled good. But his stomach didn't feel quite ready for food yet, so he settled for a long drink of water from the jug. Then he tried to stand up and immediately got the spins before sitting back down. Clearly, his body wasn't quite ready to move.

He tried to think, doing breathing exercises to calm and focus his mind. Bits of other memory began to surface, so fragmented and fleeting they could well have been nothing more than parts of a dream recalled. A powered fishing vessel—a purse seiner—towing him to a small harbor. People who looked Native American circled around and staring down at him as he lay on his back on the dock. The same people giving him water, a blanket, a cot.

Best he could figure, a fishing boat had received his distress call, located him with a direction finder or radar, and rescued him. He was sure he owed the crew his life.

"Deus ex machina," he muttered as he gazed out the tiny window, smiling weakly, remembering his late friend John Pratt. He'd explained the meaning of the Latin phrase while teasing Pratt about a ludicrous, gimmicky plot twist in a book he was reading. A happy memory. He got back into the cot and went back to sleep.

FORTY

The next time he woke it was night. This time when he sat up, he was hungry. By the pale moonlight shining in through the window, he devoured the two empanadas sitting on the plate next to his bed. They were filled with fried onion and cheese. He swore they were the best things he'd ever eaten. He licked every crumb off the plate, then drank all the water remaining in the jug.

While he felt a tremendous urge to find his rescuers and thank them heartily for saving his life, he knew he had to move. It was entirely possible that his rescuers, thinking they were helping, had informed the authorities of his whereabouts and that the authorities were on their way. He attempted to stand up once again. This time his stomach tightened but he didn't get the spins. He was stable. His sense of balance had returned.

Looking around, he could see that none of his belongings were with him. There was no additional food. No clothes other than his jacket and what he was wearing, stiff from dried saltwater. It made no difference. He had to run for it.

He slipped his shoes on, grabbed his jacket, crept to the door, and slowly opened it a crack to take a look. It was a clear, starry night. The shed was at the back of a small yard behind a simple house of plywood walls and a torch-down roof. The house had no foundation, but rested on concrete pilings that had been sunk into compacted earth. Along one side of the yard, what looked like several different kinds of squash and tomatoes grew in a narrow garden plot. Just outside the door of the shed stood an ancient apple tree, its trunk half-covered in moss.

There was no activity in the yard, and there didn't appear to be anyone awake in the home. Perhaps more importantly, there were no signs of guard dogs. He opened the door, slipped out into the cool night, then went around the back of the shed and jumped a short split-rail fence that separated the yard from a rough dirt alleyway that ran behind a half-dozen similar houses. Arkin stood still to get his bearings and listen to the sounds of the night. Each end of the alley was lit with the soft orange glow of sodium vapor streetlights. He could hear one dog barking in the distance, not close enough to be a cause for concern. He also thought he heard the roar of crashing surf some distance to his right. He turned left, heading inland, figuring it was his best bet for finding a reliable means of transportation south. He was done with boats.

FORTY-ONE

By dawn, he'd managed to hoof it several miles inland, following a severely potholed road, jumping into the woods anytime a vehicle approached. He'd also stolen a couple pounds of ripe cherries from someone's yard on the outskirts of the fishing village he'd woken up in, eating one of them as he walked, carrying the rest in a makeshift carrier he'd fashioned out of his jacket. As the sky began to lighten, he found a large, dry culvert that ran under the road. He gathered up armloads of leaves and brush and dumped them into one end the culvert until he'd built up a sizable pile. Then he burrowed under it for warmth, leaving only his face exposed, and went to sleep.

*****

Arkin woke late in the day and decided to resume his walk despite the fact that it was light out. The area was very sparsely populated, and there had been so few vehicles using the road that he figured the risk of being spotted was minimal. He could always jump into the trees if he heard a vehicle approaching.

*****

Less than a mile along the road, Arkin came to a bridge over a small, crystal-clear stream. He climbed down to its bed, stripped down, and washed his filthy, salt-stiff clothes for the first time in many days, then spread them on large boulders to dry. But barely an hour later, impatient to make progress, he put them back on, still half-wet, and resumed his hike. He reckoned he was heading roughly east-southeast. Having studied maps of Chile, he figured it couldn't be more than 30 or 40 more miles to Chile's main north-south road—Ruta 5—part of the great Pan-American Highway. From there, he figured he'd try to stow away on a southbound truck.

*****

Just as the sun began to set, he came across a small grass airfield running parallel to the road in a valley running between two long, green mountains. There were three airplanes parked in the open next to a large, rusting Quonset hut hangar—an ancient Cessna 188 crop duster painted in a striped red and white sunburst pattern, a Cessna 152 with its engine removed, and what, at least at this distance, looked like an old Aeronca single-engine tail-dragger, painted from stem to stern in a bright canary yellow. Arkin figured that despite its looks, the plane probably wasn't an Aeronca because, as far as he knew, the very last general aviation Aeronca airplane had rolled out of its Middletown, Ohio, factory in the early 1950s.

Arkin didn't see any signs of life. There were no lights on in the hangar. No parked cars. An idea took shape. He'd gotten his private pilot's license years earlier—at a small but excellent flight school out in the desert between the towns of Douglas and Bisbee, Arizona—in the summer between his first and second years of law school, as he indulged a tantalizing but short-lived dream of quitting the law to become an airline pilot. But he hadn't trained in these specific models of airplane. He'd trained in the flight school's Piper Warriors and, very briefly, in a Piper Cub owned by a flying club in Tucson. But how different could it be? These were, like the Pipers, small, single-engine aircraft. Probably had service ceilings around 12,000 feet. Range of a few hundred miles. Top speed of around 100 or 120 miles per hour. And, most critically, a stall speed somewhere around 50 to 60 miles per hour.

But even if these planes had similar performance characteristics to the planes he'd trained on, there was also the problem of his lack of recent flight experience. He hadn't flown in many years. And he'd flown very little in tail-draggers. Was flying a plane like riding a bike? He doubted it. Still, he was desperate.

He walked into the forest near the end of the runway closest to the hangar and airplanes and took up a concealed position from which he could keep an eye on the entire airfield. There, he sat and watched until well into the night.

FORTY-TWO

Sometime after midnight, satisfied there was nobody in the area, Arkin broke cover and crept over to the airplane hangar, where he was elated to discover that the door was nothing more than a warped piece of plywood held fast by a padlock and chain running through a square hole in the board. He peeked through the hole to check, one last time, that nobody was inside. Then he broke the door down with three powerful flatfoot kicks.

What he found inside couldn't have been better. Three 5-gallon cans of avgas. A book of Chilean aeronautical charts. A radio headset. Two cans of Tomaticán—a Chilean tomato and corn stew that Arkin popped open and ate immediately. And keys. Two sets of keys—one for the crop duster, and one for the plane that looked like an Aeronca. Finally, something had gone his way.

Arkin figured the crop duster might have funny handling characteristics given that it carried a large tank and sprayer system for pesticides. He decided to try flying the taildragger. And sure enough, as he went back outside and approached the plane, he could see a faded but unmistakable Aeronca logo on the tail, practically glowing in the bright light of the moon. Apparently, Aeroncas were built to last.

It was a four-seater, and Arkin was thrilled to see that the cockpit had been updated somewhat since the 1950s. For one thing, it had a radio. That was critical. It also had an electric starter, which was surprising but nice. It meant he wouldn't have to prop-start the airplane, if and when the time came. No GPS, but that was hardly surprising. All things considered, he was very happy with what he found.

He dragged the tanks of avgas, one by one, out to the Aeronca, and gassed it up. Then he went back inside to study the aeronautical charts at a small wooden desk with a working lamp. He didn't yet know where he was, so he formed a plan to scan radio frequencies for the nearest navigational aids once he took off and climbed up to altitude. That way he'd be able to figure his location based on signals coming from the nearest VHF omni-directional radio installations— what pilots called VORs. More importantly, he'd be able to find an airfield close to the Isla de los Alemanes—the Island of the Germans—where he hoped to find Sheffield.

As far as he could tell, the closest airport to the Isla de los Alemanes that had a VOR was in the town of Chaitén. But there was also a small, 2,600-foot asphalt runway with no VOR or other navigational aid just outside the small town of Melinka on Isla Ascención, roughly 70 miles southwest of Chaitén. And the southern shore of Isla Ascención looked to be no more than 20 or 25 miles from the northernmost tip of Isla de los Alemanes. Arkin made a rough plan to fly south along the coast until he started receiving the VOR signal for Chaitén Airport. Then he'd follow the signal to Chaitén and, assuming the weather was clear, bear southwest until he spotted Isla Ascención and Melinka's runway from the air.

But all this would have to wait until tomorrow. He wasn't trained to fly at night. And though willing to take on significant risks at this point in his quest, the idea of attempting to fly in the dark was just too much. He set the makeshift plywood door back up in the doorframe, precariously leaning a couple of two-by-fours and a stack consisting of his two empty stew cans against the door so that if anyone tried to open it, the falling boards and cans would cause a racket that would wake him. Then he found a spot of bare floor to lie down on in a far corner of the hangar, behind a stack of boxes, and went to sleep.

FORTY-THREE

When the crystal-clear sky was just light enough for safe non-instrument flight, Arkin pulled the heavy wooden chocks from under the Aeronca's wheels, did a quick pre-flight walk-around, checked the oil, then got in the cockpit and did his best to remember the takeoff checklist he'd memorized in flight school many years earlier. *Ok. Throttle full and free, set to ½ inch open. Mixture rich. Magnetos on. Master switch on. Fuel pump on. Flaps set to 25 degrees for short-field takeoff....*

Arkin put on the radio headset, ran through the rest of what he could remember of the checklist, took a deep breath, then turned the key. The propeller began to rotate with a struggling, churning sound. Then the engine roared to life. *Yes!*

The first thing he checked was the fuel gauge. The tank was nearly full. That would certainly get him a good way along his route. Next, he checked the RPMs, oil pressure, and ammeter before turning on the radio, tuning it to 122.70 MHz, and switching up through the eight Universal Communication "UNICOM" frequencies he was taught—not even knowing whether Chile used the same frequencies as the United States—to take a quick listen for other air traffic in the area. Then, worried the engine noise might attract unwanted attention, such as from the plane's owner or an airport manager, he quickly taxied to the downwind end of the runway—testing the elevator, rudder, and ailerons along the way—and rolled into takeoff position. *Here goes nothing.* He listened carefully to the engine as he throttled up, took another deep breath, and released the brakes. The plane seemed to have good acceleration. But all Arkin could focus on was the trees that rose a few dozen yards beyond the end of the runway. He was closing on them at high speed. *Come on now. Come on, let's fly.* The tailwheel began to rise off the runway. He considered pulling back on the stick. But unsure of the plane's performance parameters, he decided to wait, despite his nerves, until he picked up a few more knots of airspeed. At last, as he could feel the plane wanting to take to the sky, he eased back on the stick and the plane rose into the air to Arkin's great exhale of relief. Looking down and back at the airfield, he could see that he'd still had a good third of the runway left to work with.

Doing his best to maintain an airspeed of around 65 knots as he climbed into the sky, Arkin looked around to see a long valley of small pastures and fruit tree orchards flanked by short green mountains. On the eastern horizon, beyond the end of the valley and backlit by bands of purple, pink and blue predawn sky, the snow-capped wall of the great Andes Mountains barely held back the sunrise. Among the mountains, several glaciated volcanic peaks rose yet higher into the sky. Despite his circumstances, Arkin couldn't help letting himself be awed by the view.

*****

Several minutes into his flight, he leveled off at roughly 8,000 feet and his airspeed rose to 95 knots. Good enough. Eyeballing his charts, then making a very rough guess at his location—anywhere in the 400-mile stretch of land between the cities of Concepción and Puerto Mont—Arkin began scanning radio frequencies for VORs in the area. He started with frequencies in the northern reaches of his search area, near Concepción, then began working his way south. After a couple of minutes, he had a good approximation of his location—about 20 miles northeast of Valdivia, maybe 230 miles north of Chaitén and the VOR he'd planned to head for. He set the radio to 112.30 MHz—the frequency for the Chaitén VOR—and turned south. Hopefully, within an hour or so, he'd start receiving its signal.

FORTY-FOUR

Just over three and a half hours later, having flown south to Chaitén before turning southwest, his fuel down to an eighth of a tank, Arkin was slowly descending toward what he hoped was Isla Ascención and the small town of Melinka. He was out over water now, the Gulf of Corcovado, its waters shining sapphire blue in the midmorning light. Off his left wing, to the southeast, he saw another gleaming white, heavily glaciated stratovolcano on the eastern horizon. It was the very same peak, with distinctive twin rock spires flanking its summit, that he'd seen on the internet back in Valparaiso, in photos taken by kayakers who were just off the northern end of Isla de los Alemanes. It was Volcán Melimoyu. He was nearly there. But was it the *right* there, or was it just another dead end?

Looking out over the nose of the airplane, he spotted an island that appeared to be the rough shape of Isla de los Alemanes as he recalled it from studying Google Earth. More importantly, as he drew closer, he could see an organized collection of objects floating in the water off the leeward shore of the island's northernmost point. He knew just what the objects were. He'd seen the same thing before, in the sheltered waters just off Port Hardy, British Columbia, where Father Bryant had, at least in theory, lived after fleeing Royburg, Kentucky. They were salmon aquaculture pens. This was it. If his instincts were legitimate, if his journey hadn't been founded on phantoms or red herrings from the get-go, then this was his destination. He was sure of it. But now came the tricky part.

He spotted Melinka's runway and began a wide turn to line up with it as he continued descending through 2,000 feet. Once lined up, he set his flaps and brought back the RPMs. Within a minute, he reckoned he was below a safe glide slope and ran the RPMs back up to maintain altitude. Then, when his approach once again looked okay, he brought the RPMs back down. He did this song and dance three more times as he neared the runway. The tarmac began at the water's edge. His altitude was down to 150 feet as he crossed over the shore and then the northern end of the runway. He was high. But he didn't want to go around and start all over again. So he made the somewhat aggressive move of pushing the plane's nose down more than was normal, dropped his altitude, then quickly pulled back to flare for landing. The plane hit hard—left wheel first—and bounced high in the air. *Shit!* With a frantic effort, he stabilized, then settled back down on the runway. Using the wheel brakes, he brought the plane down to a regular taxiing speed, spotted a large, open aircraft parking ramp, and taxied to it before shutting down. There was no terminal. No hangars even. Nobody around.

He sighed with relief, took off the headset, grabbed his things and quickly abandoned the airplane, heading off on foot down a road that led into the small town of Melinka.

*****

There wasn't much to the sleepy little town. It was maybe ten blocks long by three blocks wide, largely comprised of multicolored wooden houses built on stilts along the shoreline of a small, rocky hill. A mermaid statue occupied the town square, and a couple of L-shaped piers jutted out from the waterfront. He went into the alleyway behind a tiny grocery store and did a quick dive into their miniature dumpster, coming up with an armload of discarded, stale, but clean loaves of bread that he quickly tucked into his jacket. Moving on, he found a small harbor on the far edge of town that sheltered a handful of fishing boats—several of them beached on the tide flat, resting at an angle off their keels.

The last thing Arkin wanted to do was get on another damned boat. But he could think of no other way to get to Isla de los Alemanes short of crash landing his stolen airplane.

As he neared the end of town, he spotted three fiberglass sea kayaks pulled up onto the shore in front of a small house that didn't look occupied. Figuring that a missing kayak would cause a lot less of a hubbub than a missing fishing boat, he scouted the area to make sure nobody was around. There were several sets of kayak paddles on a crude rack built onto the side of the house. He grabbed one, scrambled down to the shore, dragged the cleanest of the three kayaks down into the water, and hopped in. As quickly as he thought he could paddle without drawing unwanted attention, Arkin made his way out of the tiny harbor and around the point, out of sight of the town.

FORTY-FIVE

When he was barely five miles from Melinka, Arkin found himself paddling alongside a pod of fast-moving austral dolphins. There were at least a dozen of them, their dorsal fins arcing up and down, in and out of the water as they made their way along. There were also several sea lions sunning themselves on the island's rocky shore. But what really took his breath away was when he spotted a group of three blue whales—the largest living animals on Earth. They surfaced no more than 50 yards from his kayak. They seemed to be moving slowly toward the open Pacific with the grace of creatures that know exactly where they belong. They spouted from their blowholes and lingered on the surface for a few moments, breathing, utterly dwarfing an awed Arkin and his kayak. Then, as quickly as they appeared, they were gone again, taking shelter in the cold deep.

*****

Hours later, having passed two other rocky, seemingly uninhabited islands, and as the sun began to sink into the west, Arkin was approaching the barren, windswept north shore of what he was 90 percent certain was Isla de los Alemanes. In the interest of stealth, he decided to paddle down the western, windward face of the island, knowing that the only significant settlement was on the leeward shore. He doubted it was that unusual for a kayak to be spotted in these waters, and he wasn't particularly worried that someone would take notice of his presence and sound the alarm. But he also didn't think paddling right up to their docks would be the best approach. He didn't know what he was going to find.

The western shore was rocky, offering no apparent soft places to land. Paddling along, he found a cove that was at least somewhat sheltered by a narrow, rocky islet, maybe 100 yards long. Seeking out the lowest saddle in the bare stone of the shore, he attempted to land, riding a surging wave up into the low point. But before he could grab for a handhold, the receding wave began to sweep him back out, turning the kayak sideways and capsizing it. He fell into the frigid water. The shocking cold made his chest tighten, made it harder for him to breathe. He struggled out of the kayak and swam for shore. After two failed attempts, he emerged on all-fours from a breaking 2-foot wave and half tumbled his way up onto a low stone shelf, his knees and one elbow scraped from struggling up and over the barnacles and mussels that seemed to coat everything below the high-tide line.

He got to his feet and took a few wobbly steps to get up away from the surf, then, losing his balance, fell onto his back on the dry grass and soft earth of a flat patch of land above the shore. His equilibrium thoroughly warped from riding the swells in his stolen kayak, he felt the sway of the waves as though he were still at sea. It hardly mattered. He planned to lie there for a good long while, waiting to catch his breath, waiting for his body to dry, and waiting for darkness to fall before setting off to scout the island.

*****

A few hours later he was relatively dry and, though still wobbly, on the move. He could see very little in the darkness—only what the dim starlight revealed. The nearby terrain was comprised of open, rolling grassland, possibly cleared at one time for livestock pasturing, with small stands of wind-bent evergreen trees here and there.

For the first mile, he saw no lights. No signs of civilization aside from rows of ancient, crumbling cypress posts of long-vanished fences. However, as he crested one particularly high knoll, he spotted a cluster of sodium vapor lights in the distance, across a low flatland below him to the east. A settlement. Surely the one he saw from the airplane. He turned toward the settlement, moving more cautiously, pausing every 30 or 40 steps to listen and study his surroundings.

It was at one such pause that he first heard the dog. A big dog—maybe a German shepherd—barking the bark of a hunter in pursuit. It was behind him. It was coming closer. *Damn.* He turned and made for the nearest clump of trees. As he set off, he tried to maintain a certain level of stealth in his movement, crouching, doing his best to tread quietly. But as the barking came nearer, he broke into a full run, fighting to maintain his balance against the rolling swells still in motion in his inner ears. He ran straight into the trees, a branch whipping his face as he entered the stand. There, he crouched and looked back. There were three flashlights trained on the ground precisely where he'd turned for the trees. In moments, they were moving toward him, the dog still barking.

Winded and suddenly out of ideas, Arkin resorted to climbing a tree, knowing as he did so that it was a fool move. In the first one he tried, he ran out of climbable branches a few feet off the ground. He descended and tried another, straining to see up into the blackness as he began. But he ran into the same problem. By the time he was 10 feet up into his third tree, they were on him. The dog stood at the base of the trunk, barking up at him and jumping, futilely, for his feet. A moment later, the three flashlights arrived and were turned up at him. Arkin heard a muttered comment in a language he didn't recognize. Something European. The next thing he knew, he was in the grips of a stun gun electrocution, white light exploding from the back of his skull. His muscles clenched involuntarily. In his agony, he was only barely aware of falling, hitting his head, legs, and left arm on at least two different branches as he dropped. But when the current released him, he found himself lying face-down on the earth at the base of the tree, his left wrist in considerable pain. Before he could move, the white light struck again, blasting across his brain and, no doubt with the help of the bump to his head, knocking him into shadow.

FORTY-SIX

"Nathaniel," a familiar voice said, dulled as if the speaker were on the other side of a window. "Nathaniel."

Arkin realized he was lying on his back on something soft. Maybe a mattress. The back of his head throbbed with pain, and when he tried to sit up on his elbows and open his reluctant eyelids just a crack, the light seemed viciously bright. It was too much, too fast. Nauseous, Arkin rolled onto his side and squeezed his eyes shut.

"Nathaniel."

Arkin knew the voice. He panted for a moment, still lying on his side and allowing another wave of concussion nausea to pass, before he willed his eyes open once more. At first, the room was washed out in overwhelming white light. But he forced his eyes to stay open. And as they slowly adjusted, things in the room began to take shape. He was in a makeshift cell of some sort, with floors of poured concrete and whitewashed walls of old cut stone. Monastic. Despite his initial impression of exceptionally bright light, the room turned out to be lit by a single incandescent light bulb screwed into a plain fixture just above the frame of the only door. Light also came in via one small window, high up on the wall on the far side of the room. But between where he lay and the wall with the window was a row of thick steel reinforcing bars, set four inches apart in new concrete, dividing the room in half. A narrow, makeshift door of cut steel plate hung on heavy hinges at one end of the rebar barrier. And in an old wooden chair just outside the barrier, smack in the middle of the room, wearing a dark, British-looking three-piece suit, sat Roland

Sheffield.

Arkin stared, mute. Sheffield looked older than he had just a few weeks earlier. His hair seemed whiter, his shoulders more slumped. But whatever he'd been through in the past several weeks really showed around his eyes. There seemed to be more wrinkles. The skin of his lids seemed to sag. He looked worried. And sad. He sat there, quiet, his hands resting on his thighs. The long hair, beard, and moustache he had in Eugene were gone.

Still lying on his side, miserable, his head throbbing, his stomach sour, Arkin tried to speak. But his drooling, slack mouth didn't want to form the words. He took a few shallow breaths and tried once more. "Roland."

Sheffield just smiled a sad smile, staring at Arkin with visible concern.

"Roland. Why—"

Sheffield raised his hand. "Nathaniel." Sheffield was the only other person in the world besides Hannah who ever called him Nathaniel instead of just Nate. "Rest, son. You're safe now. There will be time to talk later."

But Arkin couldn't wait. He fought against the disequilibrium of the concussion, panting through waves of nausea, waiting for a lull in which he could summon the strength to speak.

"I'm so sorry about Hannah," Sheffield said.

Arkin closed his eyes as Sheffield's words hit him. For the sake of his emotional stability, he'd been doing his best to not think about Hannah. But in his exhaustion, in his beaten down state, he was vulnerable, and Sheffield's sympathy threatened to crack his hard, outer shell. Emotion began to seep though. He fought to keep himself composed, fought for the strength to speak.

"How . . . ."

"Nathaniel, please, just rest."

"How could you do that to me?"

Sheffield's head leaned to one side, his sad face betraying confusion at Arkin's question. "I'm sorry. They were supposed to be gentle, but you surprised us when—"

"No." Arkin shook his head. "You tried to kill me. You were like a father . . . ." But his struggle to speak triggered another surge of nausea that rose from the depths of his guts. Grappling to hold back the vomit, he blacked out once more.

FORTY-SEVEN

By evening of the next day, Arkin was feeling better. Sheffield's minions, who looked decidedly northern European, had delivered several hot meals of fresh grilled salmon, dense homemade egg bread, and steamed vegetables. They even brought him real coffee—French press, Arkin guessed.

At the forefront of Arkin's mind was one simple, all-consuming question: why hadn't they simply killed him? Did they think he had information they needed? About the extent of his knowledge of their apparatus, perhaps? About the extent to which he'd communicated this knowledge to others? The extent of their exposure?

Ten minutes after listening to a helicopter land nearby, and just as the sun was going down, Arkin was lying on his back on his cot and staring at the ceiling when an unseen guard opened the outer door. Sheffield walked in and sat down in the same wooden chair he'd sat in the day before, outside the rebar wall that kept Arkin contained. Arkin remained on his back, but turned to see Sheffield dressed in an olive green Nomex flight suit, his arms crossed, his eyes studying his captive.

"Nice outfit, Roland. Are you auditioning for *Top Gun 2?*"

"Your sense of humor endures. That's a good sign."

Arkin slowly turned and rose to a sitting position, holding the back of his still-throbbing head with one hand as he did so. "You know, I'm getting a little tired of you and your goons shooting me, lighting me up with stun guns, and dropping me out of trees. It hurts."

"I'm sorry about that. They had to assume you were armed. Plus, you surprised them again." Sheffield smiled and shook his head. "For the umpteenth time, you surprised them. First, you give our nine-man surveillance team the slip in Colorado. Then you completely bypass Port Hardy, where they were lying in wait for you, instead heading straight to Vancouver. I'm still puzzling over how you figured out to do that. Then, of course, you surprised us by popping up in Oregon. This time, we weren't taking any chances.

We had a pretty good idea you were in the neighborhood after that woman, presumably on your instruction, pretended to be trying to deliver a package to the office in Valparaiso. Needless to say, that phone number relays calls to here. And as I'm sure you figured out, nobody ever delivers anything to that office. So, your accomplice's call caught our attention. And then, of course, you killed a member of our extraction team."

"Extraction team? The son of a bitch opened fire the moment he saw me."

"They were instructed to take you alive."

"Perhaps that detail was lost in translation."

Sheffield looked troubled at hearing this but regained his composure. "At any rate, in the days since your encounter with the extraction team, we've been staking out every bus station from Puerto Cisnes to Chaitén to Quellón. We had guys driving up and down the Carretera Austral, watching for hitchers, studying the occupants of each car that passed. But to come via the open sea? In a kayak?" He shook his head again. "Nobody expected that. Clever, Nathaniel." Sheffield smiled a sad smile of approval at his former pupil's cunning. "I should have expected nothing less. You were the finest agent who ever worked for me."

"Don't try to butter me up, Roland. My ribs still hurt from where you put three bullets in my vest."

"You had me cornered. You'd become an existential threat to the group. It wasn't personal."

"Oh, well then."

"You were the best agent I ever had. You were my greatest hope. Still are."

"Please," Arkin said in a disgusted tone of voice. But against his will, Sheffield's comment made Arkin pause and think. "Greatest hope for what?"

"Oh, don't be obtuse. To join me, of course. Now that you're here, now that you know the truth, we can dispense with the façades and present our philosophy to you in a more direct and compelling form. I'm confident we'll be able to show you the light."

"The light, huh? And how will you ever know that you've

converted me? That I'm not faking it and waiting for you to take the cuffs off so I can make a run for it?"

"Where else could you go?"

"Somewhere with no extradition treaty with the U.S. Maybe Venezuela. Antarctica."

"Don't be silly."

"Really, though. How will you know I've bought in?"

"We'll send you out with teams for the first few missions. The team will be there to watch you. You'll be there to pull the trigger on the target. After a few of those, we'll probably be more confident that you're a true believer."

"I suppose I see the logic of that. Where are we, by the way?"

"You are on La Isla de los Alemanes in the Chonos Archipelago. And it's Pearl Harbor Day, December the 7th, in case you're interested."

Arkin nodded, reflecting on how far he'd come. It felt as though he'd been gone from Durango for years, though it had only been a few weeks.

"So, you had watchers at bus stations and on the highways for miles in every direction, huh? How many people do you have down here?"

"Enough," Sheffield said, perfectly aware of Arkin's probe for information.

"What is this place?"

"It was a sheepherding station. The remains of an attempt by German and Basque ex-pats to set up an agrarian utopia back in the early 1900s."

"So, the plan is to convert me? Wouldn't it be a lot easier to just shoot me?"

"You're worth too much. You have too much skill. Too much potential. Plus, I know you're teachable. Receptive to our ideas. I know the way you think. I know your philosophy."

"My philosophy?"

"Of our battle against the forces of darkness. You know what's necessary, even if you're still reluctant to cross the line. You're going to see the light and join us." Sheffield smiled. "Either that, or we'll dump you, bound and gagged, where some dust-eating U.S. Border Patrol agent will boost his thankless career by finding you, a red-hot fugitive, out in the mountains east of San Diego." He laughed. Arkin just stared at him. "But that's not going to happen." He rose. "So, rest for now. We'll have plenty of time to talk later, once you've recovered."

"I feel fine."

"You don't look fine. And anyway, I'll be rather busy for the next couple of days. Our pursuit of you required the dedication of considerable resources. Movement of personnel and so forth. So, I busy myself orchestrating our redeployments."

"Sorry to have inconvenienced you."

"I'm sure you are. In the meantime, you'll be well-fed, and the guards will take you out for a daily walk, weather permitting, to give you some exercise. Any requests?"

"I have a craving for matzo ball soup."

"I don't know that we have cracker meal. How about chicken noodle?"

"Good enough."

FORTY-EIGHT

The next day, as promised, three guards took Arkin on a long walk around the island. To his continuing surprise, there wasn't a Chilean among them. They looked German. Tall and blond. But they didn't speak German. They didn't speak much at all, probably under orders from Sheffield. But when they did, Arkin tried to figure out the language. Was it Czech? Hungarian? Lithuanian? He couldn't tell. But they were European, surely. They all smoked wretched, filterless European cigarettes. He wondered where and how Sheffield recruited them.

For the next several days, he was allowed to leave his cell unfettered, though always with his three-man escort, and only after they locked an electronic tracking bracelet to his ankle. He doubted he could have overcome or escaped all three of his escorts anyway. They were much bigger than he was. Plus, they were professionals. Arkin could tell just by the way they carried themselves. Where they stood in relation to him as they walked, how they spaced their feet, how they maintained a thinly veiled readiness posture. On top of that, one of them—the one who invariably trailed the rest of them at a perfect tactical distance—carried a stun gun on one hip, and a .40 caliber Sig Sauer semiautomatic on the other.

Despite the constant presence of the guards, Arkin took every opportunity to study the area, looking for the means of his eventual escape. His cell was in a small, old stone house, probably built for food storage before the invention of refrigerators. But the house was merely one of a rectangular compound of a six small houses and other structures, all of them made of stone, all of them whitewashed. The whole compound was surrounded by a high, newer looking cinderblock wall that very much reminded Arkin of the wall surrounding the late Reverend Sam Egan's house back in Cortez, Colorado. One of the larger houses had a satellite dish and several large antennae protruding from its roof, as well as what looked like a wheelchair ramp leading up to its door. The settlement and small marina he'd seen from the plane were down a rutted gravel road roughly half a mile east of the compound. There were several modern industrial buildings there, with walls and roofs of corrugated tin. Along the shore in front of them was a recently built service pier with a tender vessel of some sort tied up at one end of it. Probably the boat that worked the salmon farming pens that floated just offshore. The marina was filled with power boats of various sizes and functions— some trawlers, an out-of-place looking cabin cruiser, and one very small freighter.

One day, his escorts took him hiking on the faint vestige of a sheep trail that ran along the very periphery of the island. A half mile or so from the compound, the rolling ground briefly flattened out into a sort of low plain. Halfway across it, Arkin saw, to his alarm, fresh graves. Seven of them. Each piled with raised and upturned earth that hadn't yet settled back down flush with the surrounding pastureland. None of them more than a year old. His imagination ran wild with the implications.

He saw very few people out and about. But given the number of buildings with lights on or with smoke rising from their chimneys, and given the number of boats in the marina, he guessed there were several dozen people on the island. When he did see people, they tended to stop and stare at him, their facial expressions betraying a sort of wonder, as if they were thinking *that's the guy*. Among them, he saw a mix of ethnicities. Mainly European. One East Asian. One sub-continent Indian. Another who might have been Ashkenazi. Not one of them spoke when he was within earshot.

He tried to figure out the security arrangement. Listening carefully each morning, it seemed to him that two of his escorts arrived from elsewhere, meeting the third—probably the one with the weapons—who sat just outside the door of the house they had him in. There were two thick timber doors through the high outer wall of the compound. But, while they were barred from within as a matter of routine, they did not appear to be actively guarded. Of course, it was possible he wasn't seeing the full extent of their security apparatus. Knowing Sheffield, the compound was bound to have significant hidden defenses. All the same, the outer wall struck Arkin as perplexing overkill. What on Earth could they be worried about in this remote corner of the world that would warrant the installation of 10-foot walls? Holdout bands of Mapuche cannibals? Dinosaurs?

In the time he was confined to his cell, Arkin began to work out an approach to dealing with Sheffield's group. For starters, he knew he had to keep his rage contained. Blowing up at this point would do far more harm than good. If they truly intended to convert him to their cause, he would pretend to play ball. Only not too easily, as that would make them suspicious. No, he'd play the long game. He'd play hard to get. The skeptic with potential. It might take a long, long time. But one day, when they at last believed he was all theirs and dropped their guard, he would take them down.

FORTY-NINE

After five days, Sheffield reappeared, once again wearing his dark three-piece suit, which struck Arkin as a ridiculous and entirely impractical choice of attire given their location. One of the guards followed him in with a folding card table and chess set which he set up inside the cell before locking both Arkin and Sheffield in and departing. It was an old tradition that Arkin and Sheffield shared, going back to their days in D.C., to play chess once a week over lunch. Sheffield was the better player. But Arkin had his share of wins.

Five rounds into the game, Arkin lost patience with Sheffield's chummy, business-as-usual facade. "Alright, Roland, out with it."

"I beg your pardon?"

Arkin stared at him for a moment. "Roland."

"What is it? What?"

"Who are you?"

Sheffield sat back in his chair. "The same man you knew."

"Right. And how did you come to be here?"

Sheffield smiled. "You flushed me out. Remember?"

"Don't be coy. I'm talking about the bigger picture. How did you come to be here, at the end of the road, at the bottom of the planet, playing Mistah Kurtz."

"Does that make you Marlow?"

"Marlow and I may have something in common, at the very least."

"And what is that?"

"Disappointment with the objects of our respective quests."

"Don't be cross."

"Don't be cross?" Sheffield's comment was too absurd, his tone too innocently paternal for Arkin to stomach. He scowled at Sheffield with utter venom.

"Sorry," Sheffield said at last. Then he sighed. "Alright. What do you want to know?"

"Oh, well, let's see. What, when, why?"

"Why? You already know why. We've discussed this before. You already know exactly what I would say."

"Indulge me."

Sheffield stared through the chessboard. "What is the greatest threat to the human race?"

"High fructose corn syrup."

"Are we being fatuous?"

"Nuclear weapons."

"Wrong. Nuclear weapons are nothing more than ugly inanimate objects unless a person is willing and able to use them."

"'Guns don't kill people—people kill people,' right? Okay, how about emerging viruses? Bird flu. Ebola. Drug resistant bacteria."

"No."

"Well, what then? Tell me, Roland." Then he mimicked Sheffield: "What is the greatest threat to the human race?"

"Fearmongers. Charismatic fearmongers"

"Sounds like the name of a punk rock band."

"Religious, political, social leaders, people of influence. People who convince us that if we don't get on board with their program, that we're doomed. Your crazier ministers, congressmen, TV and radio personalities. Civic leaders, academics, overlords of the financial sector. Actors, flag wavers, heroes and superstars of any ilk. People we look up to and turn to for answers. For leadership."

"That's rather a large subset of humanity, isn't it?"

"People who have the skills, charisma, and will to inspire the masses to mass murder."

"Well...." Arkin certainly saw the logic of Sheffield's point of view.

"Do you remember the conversation we had in the DOJ cafeteria just after your medal award ceremony?"

"It rings a distant bell."

"Even though you'd just been honored with the highest accolades, you were down. Profoundly frustrated, exhibiting the first symptoms of despair with respect to your job. Do you remember what you said to me?"

"Is this going to be embarrassing?"

"You told me that it would never stop, the proverbial dark tide. The onslaught of evil. You said that we didn't stand a chance in holding it back because, constrained as we were by our rules of engagement, by our ethics, by our morality, we would never beat the endless procession of people like Raylan McGill. People who had no rules. People who weren't constrained by any normal notion of right and wrong, and who were willing to do anything. People who could inspire their mesmerized followers to do anything. And that even if we did luck out and beat a Raylan McGill here or there, it would never be enough to hold back the greater flood."

"Did I use those exact words? I sound like a poet philosopher."

"The point is that, despite the mental turmoil brought on by your despair, you recognized McGill was special. You recognized in him the key to the entire group's existence. He was the leader. He was the inspiration and the glue. Without him, the group was an unorganized, infighting group of frightened, drug-dealing meatheads, tormented by feelings of helplessness. People who couldn't find their own butts with both hands, let alone stage organized terrorist attacks or hate crimes."

"And yet despite the temptation, I didn't shoot him—even though Killick, presumably on your instruction, all but begged me to as a part of what I'm guessing was some sort of test you'd devised to see if I'd cross the line."

"Many, many years ago, long before I ever met you, probably back when you were still feeding from a bottle, I came to a pair of realizations that changed the way I view the world. Like you, I reached a point of desperation. I came to understand, for the same reasons you did, that we didn't have a chance against evil, restrained as we were by our ideas of right and wrong, by our code of ethics, by the law. But I also began to see that the large- scale evil, the truly terrifying stuff, always seemed to flow, ultimately, from a fearmonger. I'm not talking about common crime. I mean the big stuff. The belief-driven or movement-driven stuff. Wide-scale harassment, intimidation, and murder campaigns. Political purges, campaigns of terrorism, ethnic cleansings, genocides. If you follow the black, oily effluent of such horrors back to their wellsprings, what do you find, invariably?"

"Your charismatic fearmongers?"

"Exactly. Fearmongers of all flavors, shapes, and sizes. Fanatics and fundamentalist madmen who promise some form of victory over evil. An abstract evil that they convince us is embodied in some real-world thing or group. Objects or people we can take on, defeat, or destroy. It is these men, Nathaniel, who are the most dangerous, because they have the magnetism, the charisma, to organize and inspire us to action in groups. Groups in which members energize and inspire each other to actions they would never have taken as individuals. Groups that pool and coordinate their efforts and resources to exponentially greater destructive power than that of scattered individuals."

"That's the story of the human race throughout recorded history. What's new?"

"9/11."

"What about it?"

"It was a great reminder, wasn't it? A reminder of what savagery men are capable of. A slap in the face and wake-up call for a world with a short attention span and fading long-term memory. After all, the Holocaust was a long time ago, right? The generation that perpetrated, witnessed, and survived it is dying off by the score every day, isn't it?"

"There's nothing new about human savagery."

"What's new is that with technological developments, advances in transportation, greater freedom of movement across rapidly disappearing borders, and so forth, a relative few can bring disproportionate terror, destruction, and death down upon huge numbers of people. A single deranged scientist or lab tech can obtain and disperse deadly radiological materials, or chemical or biological warfare agents, to catastrophic effect. A pitiful handful of fanatics can fly Boeing airliners into skyscrapers full of innocent people. A tiny cabal of maniac physicists or government officials can up and develop, sell, or even deliver and detonate crude nuclear weapons. What's new is that, these days, a few dedicated and unchecked madmen could literally destroy the world."

"Right before you shot me in Oregon, you said it was the urgency, or the exigency that justifies your methods."

"Exactly!"

"And your group here—SPECTRE, or whatever—is going to save us from all these maniac nut jobs?"

"It was about 30 years ago that I and a handful of like-minded individuals I met through, of all things, a philosophy book club in Annapolis decided to form the group. I was still a DIA field agent at the time. Anyway, we discussed precisely what I'm discussing with you, here and now, and brainstormed how we could create a force to counter the evil of the fearmongers. There were nine of us then. We were young, and each came from different walks. I was the only person in law enforcement or intelligence. But among us, we had people who were climbing the ranks of academia, of the press, of the legal community. We even had a foreign embassy official. The more we talked, the more we all realized how important our idea was. We committed ourselves to our cause, each of us planning to steer our individual careers such that our positions would bring maximum benefit to the group. As I rose in rank, for example, I was able to pass on more and more information on the terrorist and hate groups my agencies were monitoring. Others of us pressed our message through academic or legal journals, through conventions of increasing prestige and influence. Over time, we started to campaign for the election of public officials who we thought shared our beliefs, or who were running in opposition to fearmongering candidates. We helped seed discussion groups and clubs worldwide. We raised funds for academic chairs. All to spread the message."

"What message, exactly?"

"Our message about why people are so easily drawn to fearmongers, and about what drives the fearmongers to destructive and evil extremes in the first place."

"You've been involved with the group for as long as I've known you."

"Yes. And over time, the group has grown to considerable size, with chapters and operatives active in more than 20 countries worldwide."

"Why are you based here?"

"Because it's away from prying eyes. Because there are no real intelligence assets looking at southern Chile. Because, believe it or not, we grew our initial seed money from salmon farming operations."

"First in Port Hardy, British Columbia."

"Correct. And now we have salmon farms from here to Nova Scotia to Norway. It still brings in more than half of our operational funds. When you grill a farmed salmon, Nathaniel, there's about a one-in-three chance you're helping fund our group."

"I only eat wild-caught." Arkin sat back. "What happened?"

"What do you mean?"

"It sounds like it was a peaceful movement."

"Oh. Yes, well, our decision to use force was a long time coming. We'd discussed it, really struggled with it, for years. But over time, we grew more and more frustrated with the pace of things. Some of us even came to see our nonviolent efforts as futile. Still, there was a lot of dissent within the group. But then, like I said, 9/11 happened. The great wake-up call. A proverbial cold bucket of water over the head. For the first time, I would say, we became truly aware of how little time we had left. We didn't have the luxury of being able to wait for our passive movement to change things over two or three generations. Humanity would be long gone by then. So, the decision was made."

"To start taking out the fearmongers."

"Yes."

Arkin tugged at his own earlobe, as he sometimes did when contemplating a risky chess move. "Do you read Nietzsche?" he asked.

"I've been known to."

"He who fights with monsters might take care lest he thereby become a monster. Remember that one?"

"Nathaniel, our targets are like cancers on humanity. And as with any cancer cells, if you don't kill or remove them, the disease will spread and become far more dangerous. Exponentially more blood would be spilled if we didn't take proactive measures. It's unfortunate, because most of these folks are just products of the same fears so many of us are subject to. But you have to stop the flood somewhere, or else everybody will drown."

"But the decision to start using deadly force wasn't unanimous among the group's leadership, was it? The former embassy official, the Belizean man. He wasn't on board, was he?"

Sheffield shook his head, his suddenly sad eyes looking down at his hands sitting folded on his lap. "No."

Arkin let it go. "Okay. So you assassinate fearmongers."

"Only the truly dangerous ones. And only when they're on the brink of turning their followers to violence, if they haven't done so already. Like Egan in Cortez. His vitriol was heating up. Instead of shooting pool and swilling beer down at the local tavern like normal dummies, Egan's people were practicing with automatic assault rifles against targets done up to look like Bedouin Arabs. And unbeknownst to you, they were also training in bomb-making. Add to that the fact that he was very probably going to win an election to the U.S. House of Representatives, at which time taking him out would have given his cause a lot more martyr's press exposure, which is something we always hope to minimize. It's a lot less fuss to take out a mere backwoods schmuck than it is a crusading congressman."

"I'm sure." A moment passed as Sheffield studied the chess board. "So, after your orchestrated disappearance," Arkin went on, "Killick became DCI's Director of Operations. And then, presumably, he became your executant in Washington."

"Yes, Killick, the insolent ass. It should have been you. That was my plan from the very day I first interviewed and began to recruit you."

"Why me? What made you think I would cross over?"

"Because it was obvious that you were a thinker, well on your way to seeing the light. Because of your background."

"What about my background?"

"In a nutshell, it was like mine. You'd had to face mortality as a young child when your mother died. And it was clear to me that you had a giant hole in your heart—left there by the death of your mother and emotional unavailability of your creep of a father—through which a river of existential anxiety had flowed into your life. You were ignored, criticized, emotionally neglected, then shipped off to boarding school. Later, you saw enough killing and suffering through your military service to accelerate the evolution of your thinking about death. Through it all, you grew self-aware. And you saw the cause and effect."

"You assigned the Priest case to me thinking I'd be sympathetic. Thinking it was the safe play because I'd jump on board."

"We had to give it to someone. Could have handed it off to a nincompoop, I suppose. Someone who wouldn't have gotten anywhere with it. But at the time, giving it to you just felt right. We were optimistic."

"And I did well with it. But I didn't buy into the philosophy. Then I became a problem."

"Well...."

FIFTY

Day after day, Arkin played the role he'd taken on as best he could. The angry but open-minded skeptic. Not so angry or skeptical that they would think him beyond the reach of their indoctrination—beyond hope of conversion to the cause—but not so agreeable as to arouse their suspicions that he was faking it.

Playing the role was a struggle. His blood began to boil whenever he allowed himself to reflect on the fact that the group had forced him to abandon Hannah. And when he thought about Pratt, his imagination ran wild with images of sheer horror on the faces of Pratt's little children as they stood over the bloody, near-headless corpse of their dad, cut down before them as they ate breakfast. He did his best to suppress such thoughts. Still, the memories smoldered in the back of his mind.

In fact, they were haunting him as he began a game of chess with Sheffield one sunny Saturday, with Arkin playing the white side, using the common king's pawn opening. Without a moment's hesitation, Sheffield countered by moving a pawn to c4, initiating the classic and aggressive Sicilian Defense. Within 10 minutes, Sheffield closed his trap with a rook.

"Checkmate."

Arkin sighed. "That was quick."

"You're distracted."

"I must be. I didn't even recognize your Sicilian until it was a round too late to mount an effective response. And I can't help but wonder how many chess-oriented brain cells I lost when your goons electrocuted me, and I cracked my head on a branch as I fell out of that tree."

"Excuses. But you'll have to forgive them. They were brought up in an environment in which there was less concern with what we might think of as proper restraint."

"Where was that?"

Sheffield smiled and shook his head. "Elsewhere."

"Speaking of elsewhere, how did your second disappearance fly when the authorities had no body to find in your burned down house in Oregon?"

"Remember, there was a large amount of kerosene involved. We set things up so that the house would burn down entirely before any fire brigade could get there. They wouldn't expect to find an intact body. But just to help them close out the case, I had a lower jaw bone left on the pillow in the bedroom."

"A jaw bone?"

"Altered to have dental work mirroring my own. We have a dentist in the group. If a mere visual examination were made, it would pass muster. Even though they won't find complete remains, the way we left things, the investigators will be thrilled to find anything at all that will let them close out the case."

"And you just happened to have this jaw bone lying around? In a jar in your closet, perhaps?"

"In a cigar box in my closet. I had it made up just in case I ever had to set fire to the house and run for it."

"Foresight."

"You know me."

"The consummate professional," Arkin said. "I have to tell you, though, it was amateurish to allow your operatives to all rent cars in the names of Wyoming LLCs for two different missions. That pattern jumped off the page."

Sheffield laughed. "Did it?"

"And why on Earth did you let your assassin keep using Zastava rifles? Such an unusual gun. Stood out a mile."

"I know. Risky. But when you have someone as good as Andrej, you have to make certain allowances. It's what he trained on. What he's used to. Anyway, our procedures are solid enough that I don't think anyone could track a given killing all the way back to here."

"I did."

"You had more to go on. Your own history, for example. Your connection to me. Our error, as a group, was in not considering that you could be called in to investigate the Cortez killing, even though the operation took place rather far from Durango."

FIFTY-ONE

Days turned into weeks, and weeks turned into three months. The almost-daily chess games with Sheffield expanded into longer visits that often included dinner, and Arkin never ceased to be amazed at the quality and variety of Chilean and Argentine wines Sheffield brought with him. Crisp chardonnays, rich carmeneres, bold malbecs, along with innumerable, even more impressive blends.

The food was delicious as well. Given their location, the offerings tended to focus on seafood—fresh salmon, sea bass, surf clams, and crab—but at least one chicken or lamb dish was slipped in each week. The preparations were surprisingly refined. Herb and wine reductions, garlic and cream-based sauces, spice rubs, pecan and hazelnut crusts. Sometimes the meat or fish was even brined and smoked. Sadly, whenever Arkin's heart leapt over the excellence of a meal, he was brought back down with a crash at the thought of how much Hannah would have loved it.

Every now and then, Sheffield would, without explanation, disappear for several days. Usually his comings and goings could be tied to the activity of the helicopter. Arkin never bothered to ask where he went, or why, certain his inquiries would be stonewalled.

One morning he woke up to see the Brinkman oil painting of the U.S.S. Constitution hanging on the wall opposite his cell. For a moment, seeing it took him back to the Outer Banks. To happier times, when Hannah was still healthy. Still alive.

Curiously, Sheffield hadn't pushed his philosophy. In fact, he hadn't even brought it up since Arkin's first week on the island. Arkin guessed they were just letting him rest up. Letting time do its work to slowly dull his pain and anger. When he seemed ready and receptive, they'd start to work on converting him.

The bullet wound from Arkin's encounter with Petrović in Vancouver and the cracked ribs from his encounter with Sheffield in Oregon all finally healed. With plenty of rest, solid meals, and daily walks, his strength gradually returned. By April—early autumn in the southern hemisphere—he was beginning to feel like himself again, physically and mentally, though he still grieved for Hannah. In May, the temperatures began to drop and the weather began to turn for the worse such that many of his walks were postponed and he spent long hours locked in his cell. On one such day, when a gale was driving the rain sideways against the window, Sheffield showed up wearing a bright yellow plastic poncho and holding a watertight briefcase. "Didn't want you to get bored," he said as he popped the briefcase open and extracted a thick six-panel file folder. "Here, take a look at this," he said, handing it to Arkin through the bars.

"What is it?"

"A case file. A dossier, really."

"On?"

"A Swiss. Name of Hans Vogel. Lives in the countryside south of Bern."

"Is he a chocolatier or a cheesemaker?"

"He's a politician in the cantonal government. On the rise. His entire platform is that all Muslims should be expelled from Switzerland."

"I see."

"We've connected seven murders to his cabal. One, an L.A.-style drive-by shooting of some poor Moroccan grocery clerk who was standing at a bus stop. Another, an abduction and shooting of an Algerian who they grabbed as he was walking home from his custodian's job at a grammar school. The other five were an entire Algerian family who lost control of their Volkswagen and plunged off a cliff while one of Vogel's goons was trying to intimidate them, swerving his lorry at their car as they descended the narrow road from the village of Villars where the parents worked in a hotel laundry."

"Why haven't the Swiss police taken him down?"

"The Swiss, as you well know, are by and large a nation of xenophobic crazies."

"The authorities are turning a blind eye?"

"They have the same evidence that we do."

"You're going to take out Vogel."

"We haven't decided yet. But in the meantime, we'd like you to take a look at what we have here in this file. Give us your take on this guy."

"You want my opinion on whether you should kill him."

"No. Pretend our group doesn't exist. Take us out of the equation."

"That's a tall order."

"Just try. Give us your impressions of this guy. Is he a rising threat to innocent human life? Is he infecting others with his fear and hate? Will he inspire others to commit atrocities in the name of his beliefs? Is he forever going to be a small potatoes asshole, or does he or his movement pose a threat to grow into something big and strong and terrible?" Sheffield rose from his chair. "That's enough for today."

"Wait. What's on the menu for this evening?"

"Ah! Sea bass with butter, sea salt, and capers, grilled over local hardwood. Simple, but excellent. Lisbeth usually pairs it with a nice Maipo Valley sauvignon blanc. One of my favorite meals when I'm down here."

FIFTY-TWO

Over the following weeks, Sheffield brought Arkin a steady stream of files, each one filled with horrifying stories of violence, suffering, and death inspired or wrought by the fanatic or sociopath whose name appeared on the tab. An Australian cattleman who led a group pushing for an anti-Aborigine ethnic cleansing of a self-declared white territory near Perth. A Pakistani cleric who preached that women and girls who went to school should have their hands cut off. A Chinese communist and latter-day Boxer whose disciples had killed three Catholic priests in Hong Kong. A Ugandan medicine man whose followers hacked dozens of hospitalized AIDS patients to pieces with rusty machetes. An ex-pat Egyptian whose hoodlum gang was detonating pipe bombs outside Jewish grammar schools and synagogues in Buenos Aires and Montevideo. An Iranian cleric whose vigilantes had abducted and lynched five men accused of being homosexuals. Murderous fundamentalists and fanatics. Each of them charismatic and influential. Each of them on the rise, with growing followings.

Thinking it would help improve the believability of his act if a small, controlled part of him were allowed to believe in the group's doctrine, Arkin gave sincere consideration to the question of how much better off the world could be if a generation or two of such people were simply erased. It would make a real difference, there was no doubt in his mind. In seeing this, he felt an honest temptation to destroy them, just as he had when Raylan McGill was in the crosshairs of his rifle scope years earlier. He went as far as to wonder whether the moral parameters and rules that constrained him might be the product of flawed philosophy set down by flawed forefathers who'd been attributed with overblown authority by the recorders of history. After all, despite his own strict adherence to his personal moral code, in Arkin's opinion, nobody really had any authority to say, definitively, what was right and what was wrong, or what was good and what was evil. There was always going to be some element of subjectivity. Of relativity.

Over time, the case files they gave him detailed atrocities that grew more and more egregious. More and more horrible. And as they did, he found himself growing less and less troubled by the group's utter disregard of what he'd long held to be inalienable human rights to due process and the opportunity for redemption. Eventually, he began to lose sight of the border between his resistant-but-open-minded prisoner act and the part of him that genuinely agreed with the group's doctrine.

Finally, they brought Arkin a file that disturbed him so thoroughly that he had nightmares inspired by its content. It involved a man named Uktamek Babayov—formerly a deputy secret police commander in Uzbekistan, now the governor of Andijan Province. A thug and ostensibly fanatical socialist, Babayov, as part of his brutal campaign to purge his territory of quote-unquote Islamic radicals—a label he was quick to put on any political opponents, regardless of their actual level of religious fervor—was hunting the hidden ringleader of a group that distributed leaflets criticizing the government and calling for greater religious freedom and autonomy for the people of the heavily Muslim Ferghana Valley. In an effort to provoke and draw the man out, Babayov had gone to his house, barricaded his three young children inside, and firebombed it. The file contained heartbreaking witness testimony describing the children's screams as they burned to death, as well as photographs of their charred and blistered bodies pulled from the ruins by neighbors after the police had moved off. It also included a black-and-white photograph of Babayov, probably stolen from his government personnel dossier. He looked like a rabid animal. His glassy eyes burned with evil rage, even in what was probably just a routine photo for an I.D. card or credentials.

When Sheffield eventually showed up to discuss it with him—as he did after Arkin read each file—he said, "Admit it, Nathaniel. Part of you believes this man—this monster—deserves death."

"Part of me would take pleasure in killing him myself," he answered.

"And surely the world would be a better place without him."

Arkin nodded and stared an angry stare.

FIFTY-THREE

On a gray and blustery morning, Sheffield arrived with a cup of hot coffee and the announcement that they had a "surprise" for Arkin.

"What kind of surprise?"

"One we think you'll find great satisfaction in. One we think you are ready for."

Arkin gulped his coffee as soon as it was cool enough, put on his warmest clothes, and, escorted by his usual detail of guards, followed Sheffield, out into the cold and windswept open pastures of the island. Dense low clouds rendered the landscape nearly colorless, and a gale blew out of the west, chilling Arkin's face as they walked. They followed one of the paths they'd often exercised him on, up and over a gentle hill, before taking an abrupt left. Oh no. They were leading him toward the flat where he'd seen the fresh graves.

But as the graves came into view, he quickly pieced together that they were not going to shoot him. They were going to shoot someone else. A man, bound, gagged, and blindfolded, stood on his knees at the long end of a freshly dug rectangular hole. Three other men stood around him.

"Allow me to introduce you to Uktamek Babayov," Sheffield said as they arrived.

Arkin glanced at Sheffield, his face betraying his genuine surprise.

"That's right," Sheffield went on. "The Uzbek secret policeman and provincial governor. A man who has murdered at least two dozen people, including the three children you read about. The three children he burned alive."

At this, one of the men pulled a 9mm semiautomatic from a hip holster, turned it around, and reached out to hand it, butt-first, to Arkin. Arkin stared blankly at Sheffield.

"We think you're ready. We also need to know that we can trust you."

Arkin looked dubious. "Roland, I . . . ."

The man who held out the gun gave it a quick, short shake, as if to demand that Arkin take hold of it immediately. Arkin did. He stared at it for a moment, took stock of its weight. It felt foreign to him. How long—how many long months had it been since he'd held a gun? His heart began to pound in his chest. He looked down at Babayov. He thought about the file—the photographs of the dead children, burned beyond recognition. He took aim at the back of Babayov's head and touched his finger to the cold steel trigger. But there, he froze. Pulling the trigger would win him the group's trust. That was a good thing, no matter what use Arkin ultimately made of that trust. And Babayov had it coming, surely. Part of Arkin wanted to watch him burn to death. But Babayov, like all human beings, also deserved some sort of due process, didn't he? If he didn't, then civilized society deserved it. An application of the rules that gave society its form. A verdict that reaffirmed society's sense of right and wrong. Was there anything that more meaningfully set civilized society apart from the unfettered barbarity of humanity's past?

"He won't feel anything," Sheffield said.

Still, Arkin stood frozen.

"You've killed men before."

"When they were trying to kill me. Or in war."

"This *is* war."

"Not like . . . ." He clenched his teeth, trying to pull the trigger, trying not to.

"Think of those children burning to death. Use your anger as a tool."

Arkin's heart pounded in his ears.

"Please, Nate. Don't disappoint me. Not now."

The father-figure card. How low of Sheffield to play it, Arkin thought. He wasn't going to fall for it. If he shot Babayov, it would be because he'd decided it was right, not because of Sheffield's ham-fisted stab at child psychology. Trying to push himself over the line, he imagined the screaming of the children. His trigger finger began to flex. But then something suddenly struck him as odd. Babayov's hair was curly. Exceptionally curly. Like that of someone from Lebanon or some other Mediterranean country. Uzbeks were Central Asian— mostly ethnic Turkik, sometimes Persian. They didn't have such curly hair. And why was he gagged? So Arkin couldn't hear him speak? Couldn't hear what language he spoke? And did it really make sense that they would go to all the trouble to bring the man all the way from Central Asia to Southern Chile just to test Arkin? Weren't there easier ways?

As Arkin pondered this, it occurred to him that the Babayov file was horrifying in a perfect way. In perhaps too perfect a way. In a way tailored to push Arkin's buttons. To push him over the edge. A fabrication? His gut told him it was more than possible, and that maybe the man whose head he aimed at was just some poor guy the group needed to get rid of. Maybe someone whose conscience had finally gotten the better of him, causing him to break ranks. Someone who wanted out, or threatened to tell his story to the authorities. A convenient tool for the group's test of Arkin's conversion. His trigger finger relaxed and drew back a hair.

What now? Did he try to shoot his captors? There were six of them. At least three of them were armed. And he'd bet good money that there was only one bullet in his own magazine. He lowered the gun.

"What's wrong?"

"I'm sorry, Roland. I just can't."

Sheffield looked more irritated than disappointed. And as he and Arkin stood staring at each other, the man who'd originally handed him the gun grabbed it back from Arkin, took prompt aim, and shot the bound man in the back of the head. His body fell into the new grave.

*****

Over the following weeks, the files continued to come, and Sheffield continued to visit to discuss them. But there seemed, to Arkin, to be less direction or logic to the process. For example, the horrors described in the files didn't gradually increase in magnitude or outrageousness as they had before. And Sheffield's comments seemed more haphazard. Still on point, but largely rudderless.

It didn't matter. Convinced as he was that the group had used false information to try to trick him into shooting a man, he would never trust them again. He would never join them. He just had to keep his anger in check and play the part until an opportunity for meaningful action presented itself.

FIFTY-FOUR

One late autumn day, Sheffield showed up with the chessboard, his glasses hanging, to Arkin's horror, from a fluorescent neoprene eyewear retainer much like the one Pratt used to wear. Memories came flooding in. Earnest and innocent John Pratt from Eden, Utah. Husband to Ella, father to Kayla, John Junior, Sarah and Jake. A good husband and father. A good man.

Arkin did his best to bury the emotions and focus on the game. He played the black side, and as he predicted, Sheffield took an aggressive approach, beginning with a king's pawn opening in what would develop, as Arkin taunted him with his black king's knight, into a classic four pawns attack.

"So where else does your money come from, if not entirely from salmon farming?"

"We have donors all over the world. Some sit in high places. Some are household names."

"Like who?"

"Let's just say that if it ever got out who was giving us money, you would see faces you recognize from some rather large multinational software, internet search engine, media, and conglomerate holding companies being paraded across your TV screen."

Arkin began to spring his trap, first taking a pawn at the edge of Sheffield's line. But after several more turns, despite his best efforts to stay focused, Arkin found his attention being repeatedly drawn to Sheffield's fluorescent eyewear retainer. Every time he looked at it, he thought of Pratt and his family, and his anger grew. Soon it became more than he could fully contain. He knew better than to ask, but couldn't help himself. "Did you really have to kill Pratt?"

Sheffield took a long time to answer. "That was unfortunate."

"Yes." Arkin took another of Sheffield's pawns.

"It was not a decision that was made lightly. But there was no other option. We had no time to find a better way. He surprised us. He was going to expose us. He threatened our very existence. We acted out of a greater love for humanity."

Arkin took a couple of deep breaths through his nose as his blood began to boil. If only Sheffield hadn't uttered that last, ridiculously offensive sentence. Sheffield, the man who'd presumably ordered Pratt's murder, the man who'd forced Arkin to abandon his dying wife. Hearing him say that he acted out of a greater love for humanity flipped a switch in Arkin's mind. He was instantly furious but fought to keep it under wraps.

"Isn't there some other, non-lethal approach you could take in dealing with the fear- mongers?"

"Such as?"

"Such as addressing what creates them in the first place, or addressing what makes some people more susceptible to their influence."

Sheffield smiled an approving smile. "So where would you start?"

"Identify the cause. The process. It isn't inherent or universal. After all, we aren't all fearmongers, and we aren't all overly susceptible to fearmongering, right? If we were, we'd all be fanatics or their followers. We'd all be Nazis or Earth First tree spikers or suicide bombers. So what drives some of us down those paths?"

"You tell me."

"I don't know. You've spent a lot more time thinking about this than I have."

"You're not getting off that easy. Let me ask you this: What drove you when you were a striver, working your fingers to the bone trying to climb that slippery career ladder back in D.C.?"

"Drove?"

"What were you after? You were so dedicated and tenacious. So driven. To what end? An enviable reputation? Fame? More power? More control? Your father's approval and unconditional love?"

"I don't know."

"Oh, please. You're more self-aware than that."

"I suppose we're all looking for some sort of lasting meaning. Checkmate."

"What?" Sheffield stared at the board. "Alekhine's Defense?"

Arkin nodded. "Planinc Variation."

"And I charged right into it with my eyes wide shut."

"You did."

"I should have recognized it."

"But you didn't."

"No." Sheffield gazed at the chessboard for another disbelieving moment. "Do you remember telling me about how depressing you thought it was that the Colorado River ran dry short of the sea? Why do you think that bothered you so much?"

Arkin sat silent, perplexed by Sheffield's question.

"Think about that, and we'll pick this up another time. Suffice it to say, we've given a great, great deal of thought and effort to non-violent tactics. But the sad fact is, you don't treat cancer with gentle medicines and then hope for slow progress."

Arkin didn't want to pick it up another time. He was fuming, itching for a fight. "That sounds like the sort of clichéd metaphor a cable news pundit would use," he said, knowing Sheffield despised all things cable.

Sheffield smiled weakly. "What an awful thing to say."

"If you don't like it, then play me straight and quit feeding me your abstract tripe. Tell me what you're getting at."

Sheffield held his palms up as if in surrender. "Another question, then."

"Fine."

"Who was the most evil person in the history of the world?"

"Hitler."

"You said that without hesitation."

"We've been over this."

"And yet, years ago, when we discussed this, you said you wouldn't have gunned down Hitler without due process."

"Before he'd done anything. Before he'd risen from obscurity to become a threat. That was the context of our conversation."

"See, that frames our whole issue here, or at least establishes a baseline—philosophically, ethically, practically."

"And my feelings remain the same."

"I'm not asking if you'd have shot some backwoods, meth-dealing Virginia hillbilly. I'm talking about Der Fuhrer."

Arkin decided to play hard-to-get. "Well, for starters, that would be murder, right? Technically?"

"You should do stand-up comedy, Nathaniel. Really, though. If you knew you'd be saving millions and millions of lives."

"Couldn't you try to reason with him first?" Arkin asked with a silly expression.

"Reason. Like it's your high school debate club?"

"Try to convince him of the errors of his beliefs. Maybe try to redirect him to non-genocidal pursuits. Get him to pour all that pissy zealousness into quilting or yoga. Better yet, get him a shrink and a 10,000-milligram-a-day Prozac prescription."

"I'm being serious, Nathaniel."

"Well, maybe I am too," Arkin said. And the more he thought about it, the more he realized he was being at least somewhat sincere. With the benefit of historical hindsight, he was sure he'd have taken sick pleasure in blowing Hitler's head off. But nobody could see into the future. And crazy as it sounded, maybe the devil could have been diverted.

"How could you possibly know someone's destiny, and what they would become, with morally sufficient accuracy?" Arkin asked.

"We knew beyond the shadow of a doubt that McGill was a murderous psychopath who intended to time a bombing of the Holocaust Museum so that it went off when the building was packed with African American schoolchildren on field trips."

"That was different. We knew there was a certain, imminent threat because we'd been watching him for months. But I get the impression you and your group aren't going to that sort of trouble before ordering assassinations."

"Then let's say we can know based on psychological profile."

Arkin grinned. "Profile? Did I just land on another planet? Tell me you're joking." Sheffield didn't look amused. "So—what?—you ask every loudmouth psycho with a xenophobic agenda to take a Rorschach test. And then when they tell you the splotches look like a Belgian waffle, that means they're destined to be a genocidal maniac, so you kill them?"

"The Hitlers and Stalins and McGills of the world have a lot more in common than you might believe."

"Uh-huh. Well look, I've read one too many reports from the FBI profiling unit to believe that so-called science is anything more than voodoo. And so have you."

"Let's say you could really know."

"You can't."

"But for the sake of argument, let's just say—"

"Roland, Roland, Roland. Get real."

"But if you consider—"

"Roland, Hitler was an asshole, but not every asshole is a Hitler."

"What?"

"Nobody knew Hitler was going to be Hitler until he'd risen to power. But before he did, before he revealed his true nature, you'd have hardly been justified in killing him. *Mens rea* and *actus reus*. Criminal intent and a criminal act. You need both before you can even call someone a criminal. It's elementary criminal law."

Sheffield snorted. "Don't play your law school parlor games with me. You're honestly telling me you wouldn't have killed Hitler?"

"Before he'd done anything? No."

"Knowing what he would become? Knowing what he would do to your own family, Nathaniel? To your blood?"

"You can't know what someone will become. At best, you can make an educated guess. Somebody could have an experience that changes their perspective for the better. Or they could get psychiatric help—medicine or whatever—that rebalances their brain chemistry. Or they might simply have a heart attack or die in a car accident."

"If they die, they die. What's the difference?"

"Between them dying on their own versus you having your Canadian-Balkan psycho artist or some other triggerman murder them? Quit playing dumb."

Sheffield rose from his chair, his face flushed. He stared down at Arkin with nostrils flared. After a couple of deep breaths, he forced a laugh and sat back down. "You're baiting me. Or maybe it's just your anger rising to the surface again, which would be quite understandable. Yes, that's to be expected."

"Roland, how did Hitler become who he became? He wasn't born evil, was he? What was it that made him evil? Shouldn't that be what you target? Isn't that where our conversation was going before you went off on your clichéd Hitler hypothetical? I mean, you're trying to take the path of ultimate righteousness here, right? You're on, quote-unquote, humanity's side, right?"

"Whether or not he was an original source of evil hardly matters. And it's a question of practicality."

"The morality of what you do is a function of practicality. Of convenience. This is fascinating."

"What would you have us do? Kidnap the fledgling Hitlers from their far-flung bunkers and caves, and bring them bound and gagged down here for re-education? Camp Rationality?"

"That's what you're doing with me, isn't it?"

"First of all, you came to us. Second, you're starting camp a lot closer to our side of the philosophical mountain."

"Fair enough. But I imagine that in your version of the Hitler hypothetical, you're picturing him as an adult."

"So?"

"Hitler as an adult, with his stupid little moustache and his 'slap me' face, already spewing his toxic vitriol. But what if he were an infant, Roland? A helpless baby, swaddled and napping in his crib. What if he were a fetus? Would you still kill him in either of those scenarios?"

"Without hesitation."

"A napping baby, Roland? Really?"

"I'd smother it with no more remorse than if I were stepping on black widow eggs."

"You're just saying that for dramatic effect."

"No. I couldn't be more sincere."

"I refuse to believe you would let logic trample humanity like that."

"And I can't imagine anything more humane. Don't tell me you're starting to buy into all that superstitious nonsense about humans having souls that attach in the womb. You've never been religious."

"I don't know what I believe. But I refuse to believe that people are evil—or destined for evil—the moment they're conceived, or the moment they're born. And I know for a fact that nobody can see into the future such that they can know for certain whether someone is beyond help, or diversion, or redemption."

"Hell's bells, Nathaniel. I can't believe what I'm hearing. Especially from someone whose own forebears were slaughtered by that maniac."

"Roland, who are you?"

"What?" he asked, visibly irritated.

"What does it mean to be human?"

Sheffield just stared, his mouth agape, his eyes turned to the wall, looking as if he were trying to remember where he'd left his car keys.

"Roland. Come back. What does it mean to be human?"

The only sign that Sheffield heard Arkin's question was a slight rise in the arch of his eyebrows. But he did not speak. As he sat there, he appeared, to Arkin's eyes, to shrink. To deflate. His shoulders slumped forward. He looked tired. At last, he muttered, "To be human is to fear death." Then he went quiet.

Arkin was furious with himself. He'd overplayed things, letting his true feelings run roughshod over his facade. Would Sheffield give up on him? How could Arkin back things up? How could he convince Sheffield that there was still hope for converting him to their cause? His mind went blank.

"Look, Roland, never mind. How about another game?"

*****

Sheffield did not appear for their chess game the following day, nor for any of the next five. Arkin took his usual exercise with his usual trio of guards, but was otherwise left alone.

FIFTY-FIVE

Six days after his confrontation with Sheffield, Arkin woke to the sound of the steel outer door slamming home and a gust of cold, outdoor morning air wafting over him, seeping through his thin blanket, making him shiver. He opened one bleary eye. On the other side of the bars, just beyond arm's reach, a long-haired figure with a gray Rasputin beard sat slumped in what appeared to be a motorized wheelchair. Still lying on his side on his cot, Arkin rubbed the blur from his eyes and took another look. Staring back at him through the bars, with his head lolling oddly to one side, his pale and aged face shriveled and sagging but still recognizable, sat Father Collin Bryant.

Arkin sat up and stared in wonder, half thinking he was in the midst of another dream. Another hallucination. Bryant's body was greatly diminished, crumpled, having obviously been ravaged by some sort of degenerative disease. But it was him, no mistake.

Bryant sat silent, his thinned and atrophied lips frozen in an involuntary grin that revealed receded gums and long, graying teeth. His body was propped up by wide padded straps that held him fast to the back of the wheelchair. Arkin was shocked at how weak Bryant looked. He had only seen photos of him as a big, vigorous, youthful man and had always thought of him as an adversary of terrible power. It didn't help Bryant's appearance that he was clothed in a sickly green Chinese tunic suit reminiscent of Chairman Mao and cut several sizes too big for his shrunken, bony frame and scrawny neck.

The unease Arkin felt under Bryant's cold stare drove him to break the silence. "Father Bryant, I presume."

Bryant remained silent and nonresponsive, his dark twinkling eyes locked on Arkin's own as if he were staring clear through Arkin's mind, reading his thoughts. Then, the fingers of Bryant's right hand began tapping at a keypad attached to one of the arms of his wheelchair. A slow, emotionless, synthesized computer voice asked Arkin a question that made his blood run cold. "Are you afraid to die?"

The voice was flat. Dead. Devoid of any emphasis that would clue the listener in as to what constituted the beginning, end, or most important parts of any given statement. Each word was annunciated as if it stood alone and wasn't part of a greater phrase or sentence.

Afraid to die? Arkin took a deep breath, exhaling slowly through his nostrils before speaking. "Right now?"

"No. In general. Do you fear death?"

Arkin shrugged. "I suppose so."

"Why?"

Arkin thought about it. "I don't know."

"Yet if you were falling from a high bridge, you would instinctively grab for a railing or safety line, wouldn't you?"

"I should think so."

"So would all human beings of sound mind. How do you teach them not to?"

"Huh?"

"How do you teach them to go against instinct? It's impractical."

Bryant's lips never moved as the synthesizer spoke for him. His expression remained utterly unchanged.

"You and I have a lot in common. Did you know that? Like you, I was born to privilege. To a wealthy family. Like you, I had to confront death and loss as a young child. I also had an absentee father and suffered from the consequent emotional abandonment at a vulnerable age."

"You, me, and Osama bin Laden."

"In a way, you could say that death and emotional abandonment played a major part shaping the lens through which I view the world."

"I'm sorry."

Bryant closed his eyes for a moment, as if calling upon a reserve of energy before continuing. "When I was a priest, I had an epiphany. One day I woke up to realize that the essence of my role as a holy man was simply to quell people's fear of death. Everything else—the

Biblical teachings, the counseling, the moral guidance—was secondary. What people were there for above all else—what they were desperately clinging to me for, whether they were consciously aware of it or not—was to have me help them manage their fear of death."

The hollow, synthesized voice seemed detached from Bryant. It was as if some omniscient presence was in the room telling Arkin a story of long ago.

"Death is, of course, part of the natural cycle of all organisms on Earth. But you are a member of the only species that is fully conscious of its mortality. A most terrible awareness."

"Yes."

"We do our best to cope with it. Some of us try to distract ourselves, lose ourselves in busywork, in entertainment, in the numbing haze of drugs or alcohol. Some of us pursue immortality via belief systems and symbols, drawing comfort and reassurance from religious faith in the existence of an afterlife. Some of us subconsciously strive for immortality through an insatiable quest for status, fame, wealth, power, control. By participating in things that are bigger than we are, or contributing to things of enduring meaning—great works, ideological movements, sporting events, war. These are the common mechanisms we use to kill the pain of our overwhelming existential anxieties. The pain of our fear."

"If you say so."

"To a degree, this fear has shaped who you've become as well, serving as a wellspring of your drive to high achievement. Your burning desire to prove yourself special in the universe. To live a life of lasting meaning."

"The point being?"

"The point being that, as you yourself mentioned to Roland, some of us are more sensitive and susceptible to our fear of death. And like addicts need their heroin, we need reassurance of immortality—immortality comfort—so badly that we'll do anything for it. We'll believe in anything that quells our fear. We'll scratch, claw, burn, shoot, and kill. Worse, we'll do it all in organized groups, at the direction of charismatic madmen whose minds are deranged by their own profound fear. Master manipulators who promise to deliver us from evil. Who promise us salvation. Who promise us some form of immortality in exchange for our devotion to the cause, however many innocent lives may be destroyed by it. However likely it is that the cause may encompass our doom as a species."

Arkin poured himself a cup of water from his porcelain pitcher as he listened. *Preachers gonna preach*, he thought.

"The irony, of course, is that it is our very fear of death that is driving us toward death. Toward the death of our species. Toward our own extinction."

"And so, because of the threat they pose, as these manipulators—these hate-mongers—emerge from their cocoons or eggs or whatever, you blow their heads off with .50 caliber Serbian sniper rifles. In the name of moderation."

"As it was for so many, 9/11 was a wake-up call for me. I was profoundly disturbed by the madness of it. Yet I was also certain that it was, like so much other evil in the world, a consequence of the fear of death."

"But the 9/11 hijackers didn't fear death. They willingly killed themselves."

"Only because they believed their suicides guaranteed their immortality in a martyr's paradise. As we began to contemplate the significance and causes of the 9/11 attacks, Roland obtained a quantity of martyrdom videos that had been filmed by Islamist suicide bombers shortly before their respective missions. We sat and watched young man after young man, each one explaining his reasons for giving his life for his cause. And it was clear to me that each one of them was terrified. I could see it in their faces."

"They were planning to blow themselves to bits, imminently. That has to scare the piss out of you, even if you sincerely believe 72 virgins are waiting to welcome you to heaven."

"No. This was a different kind of fear. More profound. An existential fear that had been festering in them for years, slowly driving them into the arms of their manipulators, and, eventually, to their self-destruction."

"You're telling me you can discern different types of fear in people from watching them on low-budget video?"

"If there is one thing I learned to recognize in my time as a priest, it was different types of fear. There is fear of spiders and things that go bump in the night. There is fear of pain. And then there is fear of the end. Of nonexistence and nothingness. This very fear was the driving force that drove these simple, otherwise docile, even timid young men to their mad acts of terrorism. I was certain of it. It was the common thread. The one thing they all shared."

"You're the expert."

Bryant paused as though exhausted. "You are hamstrung by the fact that we have given up on nonviolent means to achieve our ends when you believe some such means may be viable."

"Hamstrung? Troubled, certainly."

"Are you familiar with Terror Management Theory, Nathaniel?"

"Should I be?"

"It notes the connection between our ability, as individuals, to cope with our fear of death and our self-esteem."

"This is starting to make my head hurt."

"If we grow up feeling safe, loved, important, feeling as if our lives have real meaning, feeling that we're special in the universe, then we're better equipped to cope with the fear—what the high lords of Terror Management Theory refer to as death anxiety. Unfortunately, the opposite is true as well. Hence the Hitlers. The terrorists. But we can't intervene in the childhood of every potential psychopath. So, what do we do? Encourage this never-ending parade of deranged and extremely dangerous people to seek long-term psychotherapy as adults? Ridiculous."

"It would seem."

"Our enemy is not something we can readily defeat with nonviolent methods. In watching those martyrdom videos, recognizing death anxiety in the faces of suicide bombers, considering the tremendous wave of violence of September 2001, considering the political, religious, and weapons proliferation-related developments in the Middle East, North Korea, and elsewhere, we realized that the world was running out of time. That what our group was doing in the way of peaceful efforts, while undeniably good, was never going to suffice, that we were never going to change attitudes and thinking around the world in time to save it."

"So bold and radical action was needed."

"Bold, to be sure. But in using lethal force, we aren't altering vast swathes of society in any radical way. It's surgical. A fine-tuning."

"Fine-tuning?" Arkin felt his temperature rise. Bryant's politician-like use of sanitized phraseology struck a chord in him. "Like when you fine-tuned Pratt's head off? Fine-tuned his brains all over the wall in front of his kids as he blew them goodbye kisses while they sat eating pancakes?"

Arkin took several deep breaths through his nose and stared up at the ceiling. Wisely, Bryant gave him a moment of silence.

"I'm truly sorry about John Pratt."

Arkin had a burning urge to throw his water cup at Bryant's head. And though he knew it was an involuntary expression on Bryant's half-paralyzed face, it didn't help that the man seemed to be smirking. Nor did it help that the apology was delivered by a synthesized voice that was so emotionless as to sound mocking. Arkin fought to keep himself in check.

"But we fight for a good that is greater than any one of us," Byrant continued. "We fight for the very survival of our species. The world is on the brink."

"Has the world ever not been on the brink?"

"Rogue states on the verge of acquiring nuclear weapons capability. Zealot leaders, religious maniacs itching to use them. A world economy so delicate, so susceptible to financial shock, debt crises, bubbles, revolution, natural disasters, supply disruptions. A multiplying population, increasing the demand for dwindling resources."

"Nothing new there."

"If history tells us one thing, it's that when we fall on hard times, we have a greater tendency to turn to maniac rulers who promise to lead us out of darkness. The electorates of our precious democracies sit ever poised on the edge of willingness to hand power to madmen who promise to deliver us from evil. We must stop the next Hitlers before they take root. There is no time for the soft approach, Nathaniel."

Don't call me Nathaniel, you slack-jawed bastard, Arkin thought, guessing Bryant was doing it for some sort of manipulative psychological effect. "Ah, yes. The Hitler justification again."

"You don't hold with it. I know. But I know the human race. And I know evil."

Arkin's facade began to crumble in the face of Bryant's grandiosity. "Well I clearly don't know as much as you, but I know that I don't hold with murder."

"Evil is a relentless, remorseless force."

"Your murder of Pratt helped save the world from a greater evil, right? You're one of these 'ends justify the means' people. I've heard all those great arguments before, you know. That it's okay to kill innocents, to have collateral damage, because you're on a greater mission to save humanity," he said, his words drenched with sarcasm.

"A few are sacrificed to spare the many."

"And you're different from all the other murderous fanatics in world history who've said the same thing because your intentions are good, right? There's no survival instinct-driven, subconscious, self-serving desire for victory over mortality in your case. No."

"You know this isn't the same thing."

"Do I? Then you're the second true altruist in world history, after Mother Theresa."

"You see the logic of our mission."

"The logic." Arkin gave a sarcastic half chuckle. "Did you know that Pratt had four children? What do you think watching their father's brains get blown out will do to them in the long term? When you do that, when you leave someone's children fatherless, when you fill their minds with indelible, horrible memory, are you really combating evil, or are you just opening the portal and unleashing new evil upon the world? Evil born in the fear you've planted in the minds of those children. Evil that might multiply down through generations and spread over the world. Will the evil of what they witnessed grow within their little impressionable minds, only to emerge to horrific magnitude later in life? Perhaps all you've really done is sow the seeds of tomorrow's Hitlers and bin Ladens."

"It's horrible. But deep down, you know there is no other way."

"No, I don't know that. And neither do you. The truth is that you don't know what your targets will become. And deep down, I think, just like me and every other driven, type-A overachiever in the world, just like all the greatest monsters in human history, the Hitlers and bin Ladens and everyone else, you're just trying to satisfy your own psychological deficiency needs. Trying to quell your own existential demons with feelings of power or control or importance in the universe. Just like all of them, you're trying to fill a bottomless hole in your heart, left there, in your case, maybe by the devastating early childhood loss of your sister, or maybe by the still painful, still depleting early childhood absence of the father who was never there for you, or who never told you he loved you, or whatever. Just like every other political maniac or religious lunatic. You've become what you seek to destroy." Arkin waited as Bryant furiously typed his response.

"If our group had been around and had adopted the use of lethal force, there would never have been a Hitler or a bin Laden. Think of it, Nathaniel. Your own grandparents, your own blood—they would never have been sent to die in the camps. They were only a few years younger than you are now. Can you imagine their horror at realizing their fate? At bearing witness to such inconceivable savagery? Picture your mother's mother, being rounded up after entrusting her children to a Dutch dairyman's family, being shipped to Sobibor Camp, stripped of her clothes in the bitter cold, and marched off, naked and freezing, to her efficiently engineered death and cremation."

Arkin did picture it. He placed himself within the scene, being ushered off a crowded, feces and urine stinking boxcar inside the guarded fence line of the camp, the air freezing, gargoyle-faced guards holding bayoneted rifles, channeling terrified passengers toward a large and ominous brick building, everything black and white, everything dead silent. No sound at all. And no way out. A one-way walk with no chance of escape.

Bryant went on. "Picture your maternal grandfather, hunched over with pain and exhaustion, lice-ridden and skeletal, head shaved, pushing iron ore carts in one of der Fuhrer's steel mills before finally succumbing to starvation and exposure on a sub-freezing January day. Picture your paternal grandfather nearly meeting the same fate at Dachau."

If Bryant was trying to soften Arkin up by framing the debate in more personal terms, it was backfiring. If anything, it offended Arkin that Bryant would use his family's story like a tool. Fueled Arkin's rage. But Bryant didn't stop.

"So much suffering. So much horror and death. Sixty-two million people killed worldwide. Sixty-two million, Nathaniel. Six million Jewish men, women and children. Twenty-three million Soviets. Four-hundred-eighteen-thousand Americans. People who could have lived good and happy lives, slaughtered. And why? Because nobody tried to stop a madman until it was too late. If only we had been there before he rose to power."

"Because you would have killed him."

"Of course, we would have. If you don't think we'd have been able to predict, in sufficiently certain terms, the murderous if not genocidal desires of Hitler before he sprouted horns and assumed the throne, then you are hopelessly naive. And if you really think it's possible to divert meaningful numbers of future Hitlers from their evil paths, then you, Nathaniel, are a fool."

Arkin looked up, looked Bryant straight in the eye, dying to say, *And you, Father Bryant, are a murderer.* But knowing that it might blow things, he didn't.

An oppressive quiet settled on the room. The air suddenly felt closer. And though his flushed skin radiated heat, Arkin swore the air temperature dropped appreciably.

Bryant sat staring at Arkin, the hand on his keypad immobile, his paralyzed grin unreadable. Once again, Arkin got the feeling that Bryant could see right through him. Could read his mind. Knew that Arkin thought of him as a murderer. Arkin grew alarmed.

Was Bryant thinking of something else to say? Was he angry? Arkin stared back, noticing a glisten of drool emerging from the corner of Bryant's mouth. Could he not feel the drool? Or if he could, was he physically incapable of doing anything about it?

Bryant's hand moved to a small joystick on the wheelchair, and with a jerk, the chair turned and rolled toward the big, heavy metal outer door. He rammed his wheelchair into the door with a loud crash, backed up, and waited for the guard to open it. A moment later, the door slammed home with a deep, reverberating clang. The Priest was gone.

FIFTY-SIX

For more than three weeks, Arkin was left alone. The growing weight of his solitude began taking a toll, and the daily exercise with his trio of mute guards did little to alleviate it. He began to crave conversation. Perhaps that was part of their plan for winning him over. Using solitude to soften him up, make him more receptive. Whatever the case, after three weeks alone in his own troubled head, Arkin was ready to listen to just about anyone—Sheffield, the Priest, anyone.

One evening as it began to get dark outside, Sheffield at last reappeared, chess set in hand.

"Good evening."

"Roland, how are you?"

"It's supposed to be a full moon. But it's overcast. I can't get used to how dark it gets down here when the moon and stars aren't out. So very dark."

He was as polite as ever, yet seemed entirely uninterested in resuming any debate on the merits of the group's cause. In fact, he made no attempt to further indoctrinate Arkin. Perhaps they were going to lay off for a while.

They talked about the weather. They talked about the local flora and fauna Arkin observed on his daily walks. They even traded a couple of Naval Academy stories. They discussed nothing of consequence.

Sheffield seemed far off much of the time. Distant and unreachable. To Arkin's amazement, Sheffield, playing white, was once again lured into the overly aggressive four pawns attack. Move for move, he was making the same mistakes he'd made in their most recent game.

Something about Sheffield's manner troubled Arkin such that he felt suddenly and desperately compelled to test the waters by engaging him on the issue of the group's philosophy.

"You know, Roland, I was wondering."

"Yes?"

"What were the best ideas the group could come up with for non-lethal methods?"

"Methods?"

"I mean, I know you said that the broad approach to pushing philosophy through academic, media, and political channels just isn't quick enough. And I can see that. But what about approaching your fearmonger targets directly? Even abducting and indoctrinating them. Removing them from society until you could deter them from their destructive course. In other words, something short of just simply killing them."

"Those are interesting ideas," Sheffield said in a placating tone that was altogether out of character. "Anything is possible, I suppose."

"That's all you have to say? You are the Priest's high chamberlain, yes?"

"That's one way of describing it."

"So?"

"What do you want me to tell you? It sounds impractical, but it merits consideration."

Arkin could see that he wasn't going to get anywhere. All the more disconcerted, he took another white pawn.

"Well, look, since you apparently aren't in any rush to let me out of here, you could at least get me some decent bedding to replace the prison rack," Arkin said, nodding toward his cot.

"Yes. Yes, I suppose we could do that." Sheffield was staring down at the chessboard, as if contemplating a move. But as Arkin watched him, he realized that Sheffield wasn't studying the board at all. He was lost in thought. After a few seconds he regained his focus, then hastily moved his queen's bishop. It was a terrible move, leaving his flank utterly and obviously exposed. Yet he seemed not to notice. And it occurred to Arkin that Sheffield was avoiding eye contact. Arkin studied Sheffield's face for some sign as to his state of mind. A picture began to form. He saw discomfort. Conflict. Regret. Then it hit Arkin: They were going to kill him. And Sheffield knew it. Not only did he know it—he approved of it.

Arkin squeezed his eyes shut, then doubled over as if punched in the gut, revisiting the same painful truths he'd confronted after Sheffield shot him back in Oregon. That after all their years together, Sheffield didn't think Arkin's life was worth the trouble. That perhaps all Sheffield had ever done to make Arkin think of him as a friend and father figure was nothing more than contrived agent handling—giving Arkin what he needed in order to manipulate and control him. That Sheffield now saw him as nothing more than a tool that didn't fit the job. A disposable tool.

"Are you alright?" Sheffield asked.

Arkin nodded, still doubled over. "Lactose." He righted himself, doing his best to slip into the old field agent mindset: icy and controlled. But before he'd mastered himself, in his rush to re-erect a facade of casualness and unconcern, he moved a chess piece. It was as bad a move as Sheffield's had been. It was such a bad move that it caused Sheffield to look up at him with a questioning expression. Their eyes met. In that moment, Sheffield knew that Arkin knew. Arkin could read the realization in his face.

In two seconds that stretched out into a lifetime, Arkin saw himself sitting before the DCI disciplinary board in Washington, D.C., knowing his career was ruined. Knowing, with hindsight, that it was Sheffield who'd ruined it. He pictured Pratt's bloody corpse lying on the floor in front of his terrified children. He saw the frightened expression on Hannah's face while she lay in her hospital bed as he abandoned her.

All at once, the levee broke. All his frustration, his sorrow, his fear, his anger, shot through all corners of his body. His adrenaline surged. He became hyper-aware, visualizing windows of opportunity closing all around him. Options disintegrating before his eyes. This was his last chance. And all paths went through Sheffield.

In a blink, as Sheffield turned to run, Arkin dove over the chessboard and locked his hands around Sheffield's throat. Sheffield was a Marine and former field agent, and still had skills in defensive tactics. But he was old. Arkin was stronger, his strength supplemented by his rage, and he knew how to counter Sheffield's moves. He wrestled Sheffield to the floor, never letting go of his throat, and slid up into Sheffield's guard, sitting on his upper chest, in the ideal position to exert force and minimize resistance. He pressed his thumbs into Sheffield's windpipe, first to keep him from yelling out, but then with lethal purpose. He felt the rings of cartilage in Sheffield's throat bend, crack, and collapse. Sheffield flailed from side to side, his eyes bulging, his face turning deep red, then purple, as he fought to pull Arkin's hands away. His mouth popped open to reveal a swelling tongue. The capillaries in his eyes began to burst, red subconjunctival hemorrhages appearing here and there, until the whites began to disappear behind the dark blood. Still Sheffield struggled. And still Arkin held tight, crushing his old friend, mentor, and father figure's throat. Slowly, torturously choking the life out of him.

Eventually Sheffield stopped struggling. Stopped moving altogether. But still Arkin held tight, staring down at Sheffield's inanimate face, wary of a trick. Finally, satisfied that Sheffield's heart had stopped, he let go and stood up as though recoiling from something repulsive. He looked all around, taking stock of his situation as he pondered what to do next. He rearranged Sheffield's body so that it looked like he'd fallen backwards in his chair as they played chess, perhaps after having a heart attack, his splayed hands pressed to his upper left chest. Then he shouted to the guard. "Help! He is ill! Hello! Help!" He heard the bar being removed from the outer door and then watched it open. The alarmed guard popped his head in to take a look. Arkin did his best to feign distress over the condition of his good friend, crouching over him and commencing a version of CPR that was, by design, just bad enough to indicate that he didn't know what he was doing and needed assistance.

This was the critical moment. Did the guard take time to call for backup, or did he unlock the inner door to provide immediate help? Arkin did his best, situated as he was for his CPR act, to watch the guard's face. The guard was deeply conflicted, no doubt aware that Arkin possessed considerable hand-to-hand skills, yet also keenly aware that Sheffield might die if he didn't render help now. The guard frowned, pulled his handgun from a hip holster, took a key from his jacket pocket and opened the door. He motioned for Arkin to get back as he haphazardly aimed the gun at Arkin's abdomen with one hand while fumbling to switch on a two-way radio clipped to his belt with the other. Arkin waited for the guard to crouch down over Sheffield. Then, before the man could register the meaning of the deep red marks all around Sheffield's throat, Arkin pounced forward, shoved the gun aside with one hand and severed the man's spinal cord by chopping the side of his neck with the other. The guard dropped to the floor face down over the top of Sheffield, his last breath leaking from his body in a weak groan as his paralyzed lungs slowly collapsed.

Arkin rolled the guard onto his back, stripped him, stripped himself, and put on the guard's clothes. As expected, he found a cigarette lighter in the guard's pocket. He dragged Sheffield's body under the cot. Then he lifted the guard up onto it, turned the guard's body so that he faced away from the outer door, and did his best to cover both bodies with his blanket by draping it over the side that would be in view of anyone else who came in.

He put on the guard's holster and gun, locked the door of the cell, peeked out the cracked outer door, then stepped out into the night, closing, then barring the door behind him. As his eyes adjusted, it became clear that there was nobody else moving in the compound. For a moment, his mind drifted from the immediate to consider the crossroads where he stood. Killing Sheffield and the guard had been a matter of survival. But his desire to stop the group, his desire for revenge, and his anger were all tempting him further. Tempting him to cross the line. Tempting him to kill in cold blood. *A few sacrificed to spare the many,* Arkin thought, his lips breaking into a sneer.

Before he knew it, as inconspicuously as he could, he was strolling over to the building behind which he'd seen gas cans so many days earlier, praying they'd still be there, then praying they had fuel in them. For once, his prayers were answered on both counts, as he found two full 5-gallon gas cans. Doing his best to stay in the shadows, he made his way around the outer edge of the compound to one of the two doors through the wall. He doused the door in gasoline and poured a wide pool on the grassy earth around the base of it. Then he dribbled a gasoline trail over to the house he guessed was the Priest's residence, sloshed gas over each window, then tipped the can over on the porch and let it run all over the stairs and under the front and only door. Taking the second can, he dribbled a gasoline trail all the way across the courtyard, first over to the only hose he'd ever noticed in the compound, dousing it, and then over and into the house that held his cell. There, he poured gas onto the floor until the pool spread to surround the guard and Sheffield's bodies. Finally, he dribbled a trail to the one other door through the high wall of the compound and poured the remaining gallons at its base, doing his best to create a wide half circle with a good 10-foot radius with what was left. He opened the door, took one look back through the wall of the compound toward the building that held Sheffield's body, then toward the house that probably held the still-living Priest, bent over, and held the lighter to the gasoline. Roaring flames raced across the compound, to the two houses, to the hose, and to the far door.

The inferno blazing to his satisfaction, he turned and ran, disappearing into the surrounding darkness. He took a wide arcing path to the marina, staying well off the road, certain the raging fire at the compound would bring everyone from the waterfront. Sure enough, within minutes, he saw the headlights of several cars racing toward the compound. Gasping for air as he reached the marina, he found it utterly emptied. But he knew his good fortune wouldn't last. The Priest's people would soon figure out what had happened, and would be charging back to the marina to cut off Arkin's best escape route.

He raced down to the dock and jumped in the fastest-looking boat he could see—it was an open-top fiberglass tender, maybe 20 feet long, with a 150-horse outboard and a steering console. The keys were in the ignition. He cast off without bothering to check if there was any extra fuel, food, or water on board. It hardly mattered now. He fired up the engine, backed out of the slip, then did his best to maneuver toward the opening in the rock jetty. The steering was stiff. Looking forward as he tried to turn, he saw that his leeway was pushing him toward the concrete riprap end of the breakwater. If he drifted much farther to port, he'd hit. He passed the breakwater close enough to reach over the rail and touch it. But against all expectation, the hull didn't hit bottom, and he slipped out of the marina and into open water. Even as he did so, he could see two sets of headlights rushing back toward the marina. He rounded the northernmost tip of the island and set a westerly course straight out to sea, reasoning that they'd expect him to go north toward civilization or east toward land. But for now, he was satisfied to just get the hell away from the island, whatever the direction. And he thanked his lucky stars for the dark, overcast night.

When he was a couple of miles off shore, he turned around to see two beams of light shining out over the water, no doubt from vessels with bow-mounted search lights. They appeared to be running out toward the north and east, just as he'd anticipated. He had to get as far offshore as possible before morning light, before they could search for him with their helicopter. The engine was running fine. But the gas and temperature gauges weren't functional. He had no idea how much fuel he had, or if the engine was running hot. And if the engine died, he died.

He took stock of his situation, realizing that he probably had no food or water on board. Just the clothes on his back. Could he sneak into a village to the north or east to scrounge for provisions? No—they would expect him to try that, and would capture and kill him. There were no towns to the south—not for hundreds of kilometers anyway. He could still head that direction, at some point touching land to forage for food and fresh water. But his chances wouldn't be much better. As soon as the group decided he hadn't headed north or east, they'd search to the south, since there was nothing to the west but thousands of miles of open ocean. And even if he tried to sink the fiberglass boat and strike out over the rugged, mountainous mainland to the south, they would probably spot the wreck, fly in their tracker dogs, and hunt him down.

What to do? Drift west to New Zealand and find work on a chardonnay vineyard? With no passport? No identification? Across thousands of miles of open sea? A pipe dream. He would capsize in heavy seas and drown. Or if the sea didn't take him, he would die of hypothermia, starvation, dehydration, or all three.

Even if he evaded capture and survived, then what? He could never go home. If, by some miracle, he brought the group to justice and exonerated himself, he could never return to his old life, with all his sad and infuriating memory.

Motoring on in darkness, he realized that he was almost certainly a dead man. But to his surprise, he felt no anxiety. No fear at all. Instead, his body tingled with an unfamiliar, tickling lightness. Before he knew it, standing there at the helm and steering his boat out into the vast and empty sea, he was laughing out loud.

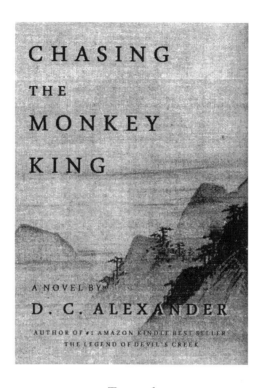

To read
CHASING THE MONKEY KING
by D.C. Alexander
please visit
AMAZON.COM

ABOUT THE AUTHOR

D.C. Alexander is a former federal agent. His debut novel, The Legend of Devil's Creek, was a #1 Amazon Kindle Best Seller. He was born and raised in the Seattle area, and now lives in Louisville, Kentucky. He welcomes your feedback. You can email him directly at:

authordcalexander@gmail.com

Made in the USA
Middletown, DE
12 January 2019